A School Called *Normal*

A School Called *Normal*

John B. Lee

mosaicPRESS

Library and Archives Canada Cataloguing in Publication

Title: A school called normal : poems & stories / John B. Lee.

Names: Lee, John B., 1951- author.

Identifiers: Canadiana (print) 20230181260 |
            Canadiana (ebook) 20230181317 |

ISBN 9781771617086 (softcover) | ISBN 9781771617093 (PDF) |
ISBN 9781771617109 (EPUB) | ISBN 9781771617116 (Kindle)

Classification: LCC PS8573.E348 S36 2023 | DDC C811/.54—dc23

Published by Mosaic Press, Oakville, Ontario, Canada, 2023.

MOSAIC PRESS, Publishers
www.Mosaic-Press.com
Copyright © John B. Lee 2023

Printed and bound in Canada.

ONTARIO ARTS COUNCIL
CONSEIL DES ARTS DE L'ONTARIO
an Ontario government agency
un organisme du gouvernement de l'Ontario

Funded by the Government of Canada
Financé par le gouvernement du Canada

ONTARIO CREATES

MOSAIC PRESS
1252 Speers Road, Units 1 & 2, Oakville, Ontario, L6L 5N9
(905) 825-2130 • info@mosaic-press.com • www.mosaic-press.com

Poems and stories from A School Called Normal have appeared in

Suffering and the Intelligence of Love in the Teaching Life: In Light and Darkness, Delicate Impact, 'The Superintendent' first appeared in the book *Into a Land of Strangers*, and then in *Beautiful Stupid*, 'Oh, my dark companion ...' also appeared originally in *Beautiful Stupid*

*"… intelligence is a weapon
best kept careful of the heart …"*

lines from the poem "Not Everyone Knows"

Table of Contents

A School Called Normal

As You Will Recall

I Can't Believe it Myself Most Days

No Time for Lies

Preface

I was born and raised a fifth generation scion of an agricultural family living on multi-purpose farm in southwestern Ontario deep in the heart of an anti-intellectual culture where intelligence and book learning were prized, though always suspect. Three of my mother's favourite phrases were "Who do you think you are? Why do you say 'I' so often? And, always be sure to hide your light under a bushel."

My paternal grandfather was an avid reader and good talker, though, by the time I came of age, he was already too old a man for me to pay attention to his erudition. I lived in a house of books, though everyone but I might be heard to say, "I don't read fiction, I have no time for lies." My mother mostly read biographies, my father was a man for newspapers and books on the mafia, my uncle read everything, my sister - nothing - and I set myself a project of reading only mostly the great books, beginning with Classics Illustrated Comics versions of literary masterpieces before graduating to the reading of the originals.

My formative education involved a three-room village school, the largest of the twelve elementary schools in the township. I started high school in 1965, attending a town school of roughly six hundred mostly rural students. After high school, I went to university in London where I attained three degrees - an Honours BA in English Literature, a Bachelor of Education, and a Masters in the Art of Teaching. In all I spent nineteen years as a student of formal education.

My learning began in the era of 'spare the rod and spoil the child' and ended in the age of postmodernism and deconstruction. The bridges of pedagogy were burning behind me while new ones were being built in my path. My last year in elementary school came at the end of one-room schoolhouses and at the start of consolidation. I walked a mile to school; the children born after me rode the bus to the new school. I attended a secondary school where cadets were compulsory for all male students. I saw that compulsion collapsing behind me. Mine was an age of 'the strap' and the knuckle crack ruler. Male teachers were often bullies, holdovers from the discipline of the war years, and by the time I graduated high school those teachers were warned off by the zeitgeist of a new more lenient era. 'Never trust anyone over thirty,' became the mantra of the adolescent ruling class.

Woolgathering

Woolgathering

in the woolgathering of overlong school mornings
I sometimes find myself seeing myself as a child
at the window half watching what I am not watching at all
there where the marbled sill caps the wall
with a slow evaporate tin trough
of warm water sitting atop
the dry-heat radiators ticking as they flex
on the floor like clocks in the coils
listening also to the drone of teacher's voice
her arm sweeping the slate
with the flaccid triceps swaying like ropes in the rigging
ropes come out of her sleeve
gone shoulder to elbow
ringing the lessons in silence
and making me wonder
what happens to women in time
and there as well
hung high on the wall
above the cracked slate at the side of the room
the black prince painted in full armour
his sword in the earth like a man in fatigue
a hero of war dressed like a beetle
dressed like a lobster
in the hard exoskeleton of the age

and I'm wonderful to be full of wonder
not quite following the plod of the lesson
chalked on yesterday's board with its P.L.O.
forbidding the janitor's will for the tabula rasa of morning

and I think of my father
as I'm sitting on his lap
and he is singing "Baa Baa black sheep ..."
as my bagatelle of trifling essentials
grows drifting full like seed kites caught on green dew

The First Day of the first day of School

in the last summer
of the final season of childhood
when we raced
in the rainbow
running naked through
the cooling veils of water
on the slippery green
of cut grass
where the redolent lawn lead
down to the wildflower fences

and all the children
were shamelessly nude
washed as they were
in the temporary prism
of split light
that lashed the blades
with a covenant
an ephemeral spectrum
of violet blushing
in the dampened air
a watering sheen
of shining flesh polished
like the patina of good soap

and wherever
the earth turned its loam
to the spade or

responded to seeding
was high country
for honey gather and
bee-busy wings among cultivated roses
climbing the noise to the top of the trellis

and then in desk shadows
we sat up straight and true
in the ultra-obedient
eager-to-please child's garden
of the classroom
compliant to the elder-kindness
of the soft-voiced teacher

though till then we were free, oh
then we were free
from the clock on the wall
and the bell in the tower
as we woke in the day like the rain

How Often I Broke it I Do Not Recall

when I was a boy
like all of my county classmates
I carried a thermos to school
which if it fell hard
to the unforgiving floor
would shatter its lining
to insulated slush leaving nothing
but a sharp thirst
with a shaken sound like crushed ice
in a jug
and you were left to imagine
the chromium shine
of dark silver shards
like fridge frost that sours the milk
and I recall
how light it became in the hand
thence to be poured
down the sink
with its gather of glass
slaking the drain as it sobbed
in the throat with the sorrow of loss
and though I'm forgiven
by cows
with their flavours of silage and grass
my mother clucked her tongue
for her careless boy
rinsing the morning away

The Sky That We Hold in The Mind

how strange I found it
that you loved your grandfather
for to me
he was a mean little man
ruling his perch with a squint
at the local garage
holding court
like a raw-voiced jay
and so
the day our school principal
came to your desk mid-afternoon
with the news of his passing
and she consoled you
with the silent kindness
of her hand
in the small of your spine
as you
sobbed quietly
at the thought of his loss
your red satin
big-coloured blouse
soaked at the sleeve
your shoulders
trembling
like the shining feathers of a crimson bird
shivering rain
I learned
by that lamentation

how love and hate
are often a river
pulling us under
and letting us rise
between widening shores
and shallowing rocks
with the sky in the sky
and the sky
at our shoulders
and the sky that we hold in the mind

JOHN B. LEE

... *the paper hanger's adopted daughter*

she was what my mother
might have called
a *hard girl*
what with her being
the first in her class
to wear eye liner
and lip gloss as though
she were wearing the mask
of a royal child of the courts of ancient Egypt
and we heard rumours on the playground
after the incident
concerning how she'd been
called upon
by our first male teacher
to pose as though she were
a figure of interest
modeling her body in art class
lying full out on the oak grain
of the big desk at the front of the room
like a cat on a sun-warm windowsill

and then we were there
in the shade of schoolyard trees
in the full play of light and shadow
in the green chiaroscuro of stick and leaf
at summer's end
and we listened to the sweet hiss
receiving the breeze
as though the zephyr were saying

what was it he was thinking
what must he have been thinking

instructing his young trusts
to trace with graphite on paper
the contours of her
small hip and round shoulder
like the story of darkness etched on the edge of light

Sinkers

in the tragic summers of my youth
I shivered through the cold blue-water mornings
of the public pool in the village of Rodney
where the instructors put me in a class
called 'the sinkers'
and it broke my heart
shattering like a red stone in hammered ice
to be relegated to that class for special children
how were they to know I'd been raised on the fear of drowning
by a family of dry-land hydrophobic farm stock
with nothing but bean dust and earth grit under their nails

and all July I struggled in the shallow end
until my feet slipped upward and I finally mastered what was
    called

doing the dead man's float

imagine a boy lying full out face down
on the inexhaustible surface
something in my body become buoyant as a broken branch
or an empty boat
something to rescue
and it proved to me then
that no one truly listens
to what they're saying or what's been said
calling what I accomplished
something only the drowned might achieve

my swimsuit burping air as I
came rolling in on the combers and tumbling onto the shores
    and beaches
like war dead or those who've fallen overboard
knocking their heads on the swinging boom on the way in
falling away and far beyond the triangular lake shadow of wind-
    ripped canvas

see where he stands
a shivering skinflint on the pool deck his rib count
ghostly white, lime white, drowned boy white

oh, take a deep admiring breath and say of him
he's been doing the dead man's float all morning
and he's become an expert
and he's better at it than anybody
oh surely he's the best in class

The Music Lesson

closed in behind a shut door
in the back chamber
of our elementary school classroom
we were
taken one by one
for a solitary performance
by our music teacher
the itinerate Mrs. Walker
and in that we were
rural students in choral classes
expected to follow
her finger
over the rise and fall
of quarter notes
blotting the staff
knowing *every good boy*
deserves favour
by heart, and with my pre-adolescent
larynx suffering
the inevitable laryngitis
of the peach-fuzz farm boy
I sang for her
like someone in a choke hold
I sang as though I were
auditioning for a barn-cat choir

oh, I aspired
to hit the high notes

where her manicure
lost itself
in the upper ranges
I sang
like a skeleton key
scraping a rusty escutcheon
in the dark in search
of the satisfactory snick
in a lock
called "please Lord
let me out of here"

and I tell you dear reader
I loved music
I lived in a bedroom
replete with thumbtack posters
that breathed as they stirred on the wall
like stray curtains in fresh air

and I wonder if the angel in me
was hiding somewhere
as voices of angels will hide
like dogs in the shade
when the light is too bright

for she gave me
a low C for my singing

doesn't she know
I've the voice of an angel

Cleaning the Chalk Brushes

i

some days
even the most mischievous boys
like myself
were allowed the privilege
of clapping the brushes
in the dying hours after last class
banging the chalk from ribbed felt
watching it waft away
in grey puffs
of exhausted dust
those small smoulderings
of thus lost lessons
charting arithmetic and
the travels of Magellan
vanishing from black slate
like the washed-away ships
of ice in dark water
or in the P.L.O.
of tomorrow, the song staff
of an itinerate teacher
lingering for a week
in the backslash of a left-handed singer

ii

sometimes
one might bruise the outdoor wall

with a ghostly breezing
like the slapping open
of a spectral fan
on white brick
in gauzy service to an absent hand

iii

I was once or twice
little lord
of the haunted air
shaking out
the dry cloth
blurring the weave
that had briefly held
the blank reminder of a janitorial wash

like the scratching away
of a white claw
become the slow healing
of a disappearing scar

that memory of erasure
come to *this*

a boy at the side door
under the spell of the doing
of that which
once it is done
is mostly undone by the doing

The Stories We Sometimes Tell

"And I put enmity between thee and
the woman ..."
Genesis III, xv

we were reminiscing
on the telephone, my sister and I
she in California
me in my study in Port Dover
and we were speaking
of our schooldays
those early times when
we knew each other best
a time before marriage, a
time before children and
grandchildren, a time
long before the passing of parents
into the ether of ancestors
far past this hour of ghost graves
for all the then living village

and she told a story
of how the schoolyard brat
DickyLewylle
had dropped a snake
inside the nape of her dress
so it went
essing down her spine
slithering in gingham

to where it pooled
in the small of her back
coiling where her dress
was cinched by a ribbon

and she refused to give him
the satisfaction
she simply untied the belt
of her garment
and let the serpent
drop to the earth
as it might
from the branch of a tree
and thence
through a shiver of grass
to be gone at her feet
the snake breezing
into the green shelter
of photosynthetic darkness
like the breath of an ancient sorrow
and how different
are daughters from mothers
I thought

consider the day
when little Irene Busteed
wept all morning
because bad boy Dell
had placed an earthworm
in her pencil box

and I thought also
of our father as a boy
with a rat
in his pant leg
how he'd caught it there
in his slack-legged trousers
and squeezed
until it was a dead thing
dropping like fruit spoil
into the cow flap
of the gutter at the barn

and wasn't it me
listening, with nothing to tell
but other people's stories
with a thought for the snake
and a thought for the worm
and a thought
for the rat in the straw

The Other Place

one of my grade two classmates
was a butcher's daughter
and I remember receiving a get-well-soon card she sent
to soothe me in my illness
when I was a convalescent lad
lying in a fever bed
at home in the pneumococcal mid-day darkness
of my own first short-breathed winter
where in my seventh year of life
I suffered
the medicinal-flavoured bulb end
of calibrated glass
held under the tongue
to see the mercury climbing beyond the safe numbers
well past normal
into the furrow-brow worry of
my mother's face, her hand
flacking the result
striking it against her palm
as you might a pen not working
praying for it to return to the cool zone
and I took heart
from her adult concern
I also remembered how it felt to be me
months later as a boy coming into summer
when we heard the news at school
of my young friend's father suddenly passing
and he left the world

when his heart had exploded like a struck rose
a crimson detonation in his breast
bursting the chambers and
breaking the valves
exchanging light for shadow
as it is with shade when storm winds
exhaust hot still weather

and I thought a thought
for her today, my schoolmate
orphaned so young

how I worked on in the heat of August
in the fragrance of second-cut hay
standing on stubble turning the row
with a slow pitchfork
careful of the flowers on the clover
their pleasant perfume on the stem
and I worked there in what we called
the slaughterhouse field even on kill day
when you might smell blood on the breeze
a thin red scent lingering in the torpor
and you wanted to be forgiven
for being human
you longed to be seeing your face
as a washing away meander
in the crimson-beribboned water
of the creek
and you say there as you might have said on Sunday

this is my blood which is shed for you

and you look at yourself there
in the burning heaven blooming blue above the harvest
and you long to know
how moon–memory and remindful sun
might become a cloth to cool the mind
of the child within the man

First Communion

When the married priest
taught us the Ten Commandments
in Catechism class
in preparation for Confirmation
and the transubstantiation
of First Communion
he told his ten year old tribe
of supplicants
if we dared to defy
the eighth commandment
the one on the second tablet
shattered at the feet of Moses
come down from the mountain of terror
his wild hair floating
his white beard raging like cloudburst
storming at the feet of the golden calf
that if we dared defy God
committing *adultery*
(whatever that was)
our flesh would be scabbed with pox
our noses grow rotten
and fall away from our faces
leaving two black holes in swathing
like Boris Karloff in *The Mummy*
and our minds
would be eaten away by slow madness

and then on the day
of the first receiving of the consecrated host

that thin wafer of flesh tasting
like a small wedge of uncooked pie
stolen from the crimped rim of the pan
unleavened and doughy on the tongue
followed fast
by the first bitter-sweet sip
of holy wine with a warm swallow of fermented grape
going down the throat in a gentle burn
we boys and girls kneeling
in a sinning crush
of crinoline and knee-creased wool
the girls flour dusted to the wrist in white-lace gloves
the soles of their new shoes shining
in the sacramental Sunday of our youth
wondering about the mysteries of the night
pouring like gold in miraculous form in secret places
forbidden by hands upon bodies touched by fire

JOHN B. LEE

The Superintendent

who does not fear

or loathe to hear
the superintendent of schools
with her disapproving
and ultra-grammatical
crepitation, clearing her throat
with a phlegmy "ahem"
from the back of the room
her spine as stiff as a pointer
she strides
her heels cracking the floor
as she seizes the chalk of the day
and with white streak
screeching

is it a sin or is it a dream of sin
to see through the third eye
how the children tremble
shading their work
for a smudge of errors
the grand failures
we feel in the pedagogical squint
of the once-a-term stranger
in a classroom smelling of spilled ink
and the bass notes of old plasticine
fragrant in bent fingers
and multi-coloured snakes of clay

rolled flat on the modeling board
one name carved deep
in the cave of every desk

for we are the bullied, the shy
the wild, the plump
the brilliant, the lost
the bratty, the eager-to-please
the quiet, the pimpled
the unclean, the poor
the criminal, the crippled, the maimed
the doomed-to-die young
the bad seed, the sniffling, sniveling
easy-to-hate tattletale
the pampered
the beaten, the bewildered
the too-stupid-for words
learning one lesson in a tall cone-shaped hat
under tousled hair

and one in the tasseled
mortarboard

we all share our nature with the dead
one name carved deep in the cave
of every empty desk is yours
and one name there is mine

Oh, my dark companion ...

my sister tells me the story
of how
when she was a girl
she witnessed the arrival
at the girls' door of SS No. 6
the village elementary school
we attended as children
and she and her friends
watched as Miss Myrtle Downie
walked up to unlock the building
as was her morning practice
and there
sheathed over the handle
some local wag
had affixed an unused prophylactic
skinning the knob
like a blister on brass
and she peeled the latex
as an audience giggled shyly behind their hands
placed the safe to her lips
and inflated the thing
as though she were about to amaze them all
with a poodle balloon

and I thought as the tale unfolded
how some rough-living prankster
some nearly-shaving rogue
some going-on-for-sixteen quitter

might have been there
secreted nearby and hiding behind
one of the *pump-pump pole away* maples
those tag-and-your *it* trees
that framed our play
where we stood in captivity
holding each other hand to hand
like a string of paper dolls

I almost hear
the stifling of raw laughter
red-faced and mean-spirited
guffaws like an old man coughing

and our school marm placed
the filmy inflation
taking in a last big breath
like final wishes
as the milk-film translucence of that small zeppelin
filled her hands
and I cherish the charm of the virgin
the life-long chastity
of that dear woman
for whom we were all of us
her beloved children - every one
and I do not laugh
but smile

if I think
how last evening
in a poets' circle

we talked of Sir William Osler
that nineteenth century physician
who encouraged his medical students to pursue
a clear mind and
a loving heart
he who first saw
animalcules flowering on filmy glass
he who studied cadavers in the dead house
within the courtyard of the Blockley gardens
alive with yellow daffodils
in the Cotswold village
beside the pond
where the bronze statue of a young girl
pours out unceasing waters
from giving jug to
ever-receiving rippling pool

and if there is life eternal
in Osler's ashes
at old McGill
where all the equanimities
of one soul
radiate like the bell
we once heard
sounding over the land of our youth
calling us to attend
and give
obeisance to lost memory
as all learning *is* quintessential recall
of the already known

is it little wonder then
that I give Christ's benefit
to the lascivious and seemingly snide youth
hiding in the shadows of time
like everyone's dark companion

A Secret We'd Never Tell

we were three boys
near the bent-by-climbing
fence line crumpled on the green
perimeter at the back of the schoolyard
out where the bell sound
thinned to a lessening gong
in the wether-shadow
of gorse in tall grass
where the spring water
set its evaporate
looking glass in post rot
and it was pollywog busy
for the jam-jar interest
of youth
and I somehow needled
my best friend's brother
so he reached
for a close-at-hand weapon
a tossed-away short stud club
which he swung in the air
like a battlefield cudgel
a killer's swipe with one carpenter's nail
fanged in the lumber
and it buzzed against bone
it caught where it rang
at the nerve ends
of arm and elbow - and
he dropped it

in hot-pipe disbelief at himself
oh *fratricide,* oh
Biblical moral of Caine - oh
brother, how I laughed
at the hurt of it
and we three boys
tumbled together in mirth
like alpha-male wolf cubs

and Miss Myrtle Downie
rocked from her shoes by the bell rope
as we raced with a secret we'd learned
something we'd never tell
not even to ourselves ...

Simplicity Itself

"I hated fractions, anything
in halves or quarters or thirds
fractured numbers, divisions, broken bits
chaos masquerading behind logical forms"
Marty Gervais from his poem "Geometry of Talk

my sister
two years my elder
is struggling with fractions
she cannot seem to comprehend
division as invert and multiply
how can it be

that such a small number
yield a larger
and my mother is with her there
at the table
in the dining room
near the parlour on the farm
and they struggle together
mystified and quarrelling
with the logic

it can't be true, it
just cannot be so — and
it doesn't make sense
this sad arithmetic
eviscerated on the maple tabletop

like the grain crop
counted out in taxes for the coffers of a king

and so
I try to help
I come to them
with an apple and a knife
like my father cutting portions at the barn
and I say *see*
if I cut the apple in two
I have a larger number
each one accounting for
a smaller portion of the whole

and then in fourths
and then in sixths and
then in eighths and
so on — simplicity itself
how many apple wedges
lighter than the last in equal portions
and yet each is one eighth
of the whole — to make the number 8

you're so stupid, that
doesn't make any sense at all

and so I am dismissed
like the waving away
of fruit flies from the bowl
and I leave them to their quarrel
like counting the coin

and seeing one hundred copper pennies
flashing to the floor
some tarnished over time
some shining each one an equal value to itself
like comparing the meaning of the heartbeat
to the meaning of the heart

What Winters in Me is the Spring

we played chatterbox at school
that fortune teller origami
a whirlybird
of paper colours and numbers
and imaginary names
flashing in the hands
of a classmate — I also almost
believed in the possibility
of truth in playing cards
turned from the pack to the light
by my beloved aunt
amusing my cousins and me
on Sundays
her cheap bracelets
jangling like candy-coloured
moon rings
sliding elbow to hand
catching the motion
of her shuffling arm
settling like abacus
on the halo-nimbus knob of her wrist
seeing my future there
in a chance encounter
of knaves and aces
Queens and Kings and
with a two-hearted vision of whom I might meet
on the road leading away from tomorrow

and one night
we played Ouija
feeling the small delicate legged
planchette slipping over the board
like the tilting of mercury spilling *this-way that-way*
our fingertips light as sparrow bone
beware of the bad spellers
shivering over the alphabet
into the nether world
where ghost shadows shimmer and gutter
like dark winds in the oak shade of streetlamps

and now
I look back over life
more memory than dream
and even though
I remain full of wonder
recollecting the seasons
as seeds in an apple
climb to the drop-down of autumn
when the sheep on the farm
came rolling their jaws
on the windfalls
in the cider-stained grass
what winters in me
is the spring
and the sorrows that blossom

Ode on a Chipped Tooth

the door at the schoolhouse
in the village
opened out
onto the playground
and it was
one brown slab
of blind wood
through which we
who were exiting
were born into the day
come out of a common darkness
and we who entered
went in
at our own peril
fresh from blue weather
and windy sway
and so I was arriving
as Leonard was leaving
both of us
in a rush to be out
or in
as was our will of wishes
and he, the happy-go-lucky
lad with a bat
on his shoulder
Ali Oop of the baseball diamond
and I
in open-mouth delight

saw him
pivot and swing –
me taking the full in the face force
of that unintended cudgel
felt the crack of the ash
as I bit
into the scorched logo
suddenly one tooth short of a smile
my incisor like a fragment of china
forever lost
I spit into my hand the hard white shard

and my friend
wept as he stood
in the aftermath
at teacher's desk
taking her reprimand
for his unintended carelessness
as we are all of us
sometimes carefree
and swinging
out into the vacancy

A School Called Normal

Accustomed as she was to her father spitting on the floor at home, my aunt, his daughter, would give my city cousins instruction to lay day-old newspapers openly scattered on the broadloom about the easy chair where he would sit whenever he came to town for a visit. And he was my paternal grandfather, my very first teacher. From him I learned to say aloud the name *A-ris-to-phanes,* from him I learned my alphabet; from him I learned to write my name in cursive; from him I learned the art of drawing a chalk-line pig, a cartoon York replete with nostrils and a curly tail. My parents had purchased a blackboard that they'd hung on the wall just outside the washroom door at the end of the kitchen. Every day after breakfast he would stop in passing and say to me, "Johnny, would you like me to draw you a pig?" Or he would print the name ARISTOPHANES in bold letters, and importune my little self to sound out the syllables, to which I would reply "Air-iss-toe-fanes" and he would greet my pronunciation with gales of laughter.

"I speak a little Chinese," he would say. "Chum-tie cumalung-tie cocka-wee-wee," all the time chortling much to his own amusement. For the longest while I thought that I too spoke a little Chinese. Since my great-aunt Ida having been a missionary in the Orient, I saw no reason that a farmer toiling the earth in southwestern Ontario would not indeed, as he'd said, "speak a little Chinese."

So, by the time I started elementary school, I already knew my alphabet, and in addition to being able to print out and recognize the entire twenty-six letters in a clear hand, I could also write my name in cursive. Why then, would little Johnny expect anything other than praise and encouragement in the classroom? Then I met Mrs. Cross. The always angry, ever exasperated grandmother of missionary children in Angola. She had the rinsed blue hair of a fairy. As I recall her, she wore those coffee mug shoes with heels like cheap cafeteria ceramics. Brown shoes laced to the ankles, serviceable, sensible shoes that struck the floor like gavels in judgment with every step she took.

I sat in the middle row, four desks from the front. The boy behind me, a lad named Bradley Wart, who wore old fashioned tortious-shell owl-rimmed spectacles, short trousers held up by clip-on suspenders, high-top farm shoes, socks almost to the knee, and homespun hair festooned by a cowlick that feathered his crown like frayed wire, a disobedient crop, a wide-nostril lad taking oxygen in loud huffs, poking me in the back with his pencil whispering "I'm your best friend, ain't I?" perseverating like a house fly on a windowpane. Eventually, I'd had enough of being spiked in the spine, so I turned around and hoping to end his hijinks, said "yes, okay, I'll be your best friend." At which point he proceeded to stab me in the fat on my hand with his sharpened pencil, thereby imbedding a pepper speck of graphite in the heel of my palm, a black dot that I can see to this day, evidence of things to come.

My school days began in the dying throes of the last decade of the *spare the rod spoil the child* credo that infected both the halls of learning and the hearth of domesticity. If you got the strap at school from teacher, you got worse at home from father. A belief in the positive affect of corporal punishment was the central tenet both of pedagogy and of parenting. For every Wackford Squeers in the classroom, there existed a Simon Legree of the parlour. If teacher lashed your hand at school, your father wielded a belt on your bare buttock at home. This hard moral, this seemingly Draconian punishment meant improvement, silence, co-operation, compliance, and a meek acquiescence to adult discipline for the owner of red palm and of welted bum. Surely you would learn your lesson and colour between the lines and follow the print with your fingertip and sharpen your pencil only when necessary and read quietly and behave, behave, behave. Sit down and behave. Oh to be one of the goody two shoes Miss Ditto schoolgirls. Oh to be Marvin Milquetoast bent meekly over his pages like a lamb at oats. Unfortunately for me, I was something of a wild child. A feral boy. I had such mischief in me that it giggled up from the floor going toe to forehead belching out of every pore like the daily repetition of the taste of cod liver oil erupting from the belly as it was with the burping of lava from an old Vesuvius event of the newest earth.

So when I was stabbed in the palm, I cried out like Caesar on the steps of the Senate. And teacher turned, her face red with rage, demanding "Who?" Bradley Wart, he of the owl-rim glasses and short-pant braces, happily identified me as the guilty party. He pointed my way as though he had played no part in my crying out. Mrs. Cross stamped her foot, crooked her finger, walked to her oaken desk, opened the drawer and drew forth what looked for all like a beavertail scabbard hanging from her arm at her side. I stood and walked and held my hand palm out, open to the ceiling, for this was not the first occasion of my receiving the windmill arm with its singing leather stinging down upon my hot flesh.

Mrs. Cross didn't like the way I sang *Jesus Loves Me* with too much enthusiasm. She took exception to the my getting up from my desk during lunch having fashioned a pair of wax-paper horns from my sandwich wrap, racing around the room goring the girls. She disapproved of my provoking one of the grade eight boys, having thrown an icy snowball at Alvin, the nystagmus-afflicted albino criminal with wiggling eyeballs, that frozen sphere striking him in the back, so he turned upon me and stuffed me at the mouth like a plaster cast so I choked and sputtered and almost died for want of oxygen. "Who threw the snowball?" was all she wanted to know. The day I swatted a bee inside Toad Henry's T-shirt so it stung and sent him screaming to tattle, or the worst day of all, the day my best friend Dicky and I took the strap out of the desk, lined up the girls, and played "pretend it was you" as one by one they came forward until Mrs. Cross stood in the doorway steaming at her nose like a horse in winter.

One day Bradley prodded me, prodded me, prodded me, perseverating "Who's your girlfriend, I won't tell." I confessed a crush on a certain girl and he immediately raced across the yard to inform the very girl who made me blush to even hear her name aloud. I was mortified. To punish myself I went inside where all student presence was forbidden during recess. I hid behind a swung open door and smashed my lunch, squeezing the fruit and kneading the doughy sandwiches so the pong of peanut butter and cold clabber seeped out of the darkness and smouldered into the light like something burning slow. "What's this then? You'll be seeing the principal and she can deal with you."

And so I entered the upper form, quivering like the breaking of a fever after a long illness. Surely, thought I, if Mrs. Cross's punishment was not sufficient to the crime, then her superior might hurt me almost unto death.

"Why are you here, dear?" she inquired.

I told her. I didn't rat on the ratfink. I didn't tell her the whole story. I simply told her that a girl knew that I loved her and the mortification of that revelation was too great a burden to bear.

"Oh, is that all? Well, we know you love everyone, don't you. We all love everyone. You're a very special boy. I think Janet knows that. Now, here, have half my sandwich, for you must eat to keep your strength up."

★

Two years hence I found myself in a very different classroom under the tutelage of a first-year teacher fresh out of Normal School. Miss Ford was doughy and plump with Queen Anne calves the colour and consistency of pork sausage. Her fat feet were stuffed in mules, the colourless flesh larding out of the leather like squeezed margarine. Not to be cruel, but she was uncommonly homely. The dark hollow of her nostrils flared like those of a skittish horse as with each breath she took in a startlement of oxygen as though she were sliding on ice. She suffered from the garlic and spice halitosis of a meat shop cold cut counter, and she had what my sister referred to as B.O. a-plenty. Though quite young, barely out of her teens, she stank of old clothes wintering in a closet, mothballs, attic trunks, and laundry left to do in a pile on the floor. When she removed her grey-wool jacket, thereby revealing her white cotton blouse with its unmatched buttons, she exposed the place where the fabric was stained yellow as old ivory giving off a fragrance of worry and the ill-at-ease stink of a nervous disposition. When she came close, you could close your eyes and imagine poor hygiene perfumed by cheap soap. She wore unfashionable cats-eye spectacles with cloudy lenses, her eyebrows shooting up into her forehead like black marks shaped by a pencil impression held by a hand on the arm of a knocked elbow. She was full cap-a-pied with good intentions. Earnest and sincere, she longed to be liked and meant to be kind, though she was incompetent at both human sympathy and likeable charm.

One thing for which we were all most grateful involved that fact that she was the first of a generation refusing to use the strap to achieve discipline. And so we became unruly, undisciplined, erasable, ungrateful, and wild.

As You Will Recall

The Shaming of George Crombez

our grade nine homeroom teacher
was a stickler
when it came to personal hygiene
every morning
from the first day forward
we'd sit at our desks
for inspection
spine straight
palms flat to the little
ink-well learning tables
and she would walk
up and down the rows
glancing at knuckles
and nails
of the predominantly farm kid
crop - and we
who worked at the barn
and in the fields
were mostly safe and
bitten to the quick
and scrubbed raw
but for one particular boy
whose hands were soiled
and whose nails
would never pass muster
for they were
uncommonly long and
they were

black with grit
and she lifted his hand
to the light
like sliver work
turning them over and back
as though with the slow
forensics of a dead coal miner's
manicure – and she
shamed him among us
she culled him as one might cull a runt
so he leapt to his feet
and ran from the room
sobbing with mortification

and it was
the year of Beatle boots
and fake medallions
with the last remaining
war-hero pedagogues
strutting the front of the room
with this English teacher
sniffing the air for body odour
as though we weren't
come in from the barn
come up from the field
children bathed in washtubs
washed in the rumours of straw
and the fragrance of home
which was wood smoke
and tallow and
mothers who loved us with soap

A Pillow Fight in Paris

when I was a boy in grade nine
I developed
a very painful boil
on the right cheek of my gluteus maximus
an excruciating furuncle
forming a fully enraged pustule
infected by staphylococcus aureus
swollen for deep weeks with dead matter
from folliculitis
which finally departed from the language
of medical Latin
suffering itself to a white *yelp*
the day it shaped its red tip
to a sharp Vesuvius
a hot peak of yellow anguish
which suddenly burst erupting in crimson gore
that spread its wet warmth
suppurating on the seat of my blue trousers
it soaked my pocket
like the sacrificial red of a lamb stone
oh – what relief
after the seemingly eternal agony
of sleepless nights lying on one side
and endless days seated at a slant
canting for mercy on the hard-bottomed torture of a
    schoolroom chair
tilting as though I were dozing or drunk

and not until yesterday
fifty years since then
have I thought of that mortification
as I fled the gymnasium
for fear that someone might see my shame
hiding my blood-soaked self
sidling along the wall with my backside to the brick
and then rushing fanny first out the door and down the street
to my grandparents' house

not until yesterday
did I give a thought of compare
to the accidental menses of a girl
spotting her skirt
as though she were wounded
her flight in tears
retiring to the red tent in the desert

and for some strange reason
it also occurred to me
to remember
the Beatles in pajamas
having a pillow fight
in a hotel room in Paris
the night they learned
they'd just achieved their first number one
in America

and they were so young
barely out of their teens
rumbustious and romping
in exuberant jubilation

History Lesson

Mr. Tailor, our grade nine history teacher
thought I'd been talking out of turn
and so he stopped the lesson
somewhere between *King Aethelred*
sire to Alfred the Great
whose second son Aethelweard
begat of wife Ealewith
born in 880 AD
died circa 920-922
defeater of Viking hordes
King of Wessex
uniter of England under
one crown - pause -
and we who copied madly
all the quick dates and royal lists
like busy little secretaries in a stenographic pool
our cramped hands racing
in blue-ink rivers
bleeding over pages grown plump with
writing in fear
that somewhere, on some future
occasion
the Anglo Saxon hordes
sunk to the thighs in grey matter
crowding the waves of the mind
with broad axes wilding
through quagmires of memory
as though they were wading ashore intent upon mayhem

and there and then at that exact moment
the master of the mead hall
stood at my desk
a hovering runt quivering with rage
"were you talking ..."

and thirty two pens suddenly went still
all wondering - perhaps
for the first time -
what happens next

The Whispering

a girl in our grade nine class
came to school every day
dressed in white go-go boots
that came half-way to the knee
and a mini skirt close to her thighs
she was clothed like a cage dancer
from Shindig on TV
and she sported long blonde
Peggy Lipton poker-straight Hollywood hair
framing her face
wearing lip gloss and
eyeliner and though
she seemed shy
crossing her legs with a care
every boy watched her
for want of a panty flash
to think of how
she might bloom like an orchid
even in the briefest of light
and we dreamed
in our pimples
we blinked in sweat from our desks
as she shifted her body
like a bird on an egg in a nest
and what was she thinking
we wondered
making mist out of math
that came sweet by the lick of her lips

and *war* out of waving
the glistening moons of her hand
with a thousand boys
dead as flies swept up on the floor

Crusher and the Assassin's Hand

our grade ten history teacher
the one we called *Crusher*
because of the way
he once
grabbed a lippy lad
by shirt collar
lifting him a hand-span from the floor
running him to the back of the room
and slamming his body
against the wall
so he hung there a moment
and then slumped
into a moaning heap on the tile
an awkward spill
of gangly adolescence
as though from this we might infer

here endeth the first lesson

he'd also bloodied
Leonard Hearns's nose
for laughing too loud and long
at a joke he'd been told
and then Crusher Clarke
seeing the crimson snooze
dripping through the boy's fingers
as though he'd suffered the spontaneous epistaxis
of an inbred Romanov prince

he said—"Go clean yourself …"
and that was that

one time
a girl had failed
to complete her homework
and as was his habit
teacher walked the rows
looking for evidence
that we had answered all his questions
from the day before
and he stopped
glowering down at the blonde girl
her notebook blank but for what she'd copied
from the board
exhausted by math, she'd gone to bed

in a rage
he picked her up
desk and thigh
turned her
pockets to the ceiling
and dropped that clatter
so she crashed
and her broken binder
sprung its rings with a hard snap
and bit into her forearm
with a silver fang

and that was he
and these our schooldays

spent studying the moods of the world
at the coming on of war

and that was a year
I remember well
when he told us
the final cause of the first great war
the war to end all wars
the one my great-uncle Jackserved in
the one where the mad poets lost their minds
and he told us
of that single cause
how one fine late June morning
the assassin GavriloPrincip
shot Archduke Ferdinand

thus setting in motion in a single month
all the bellicose armies of Europe

and now
as we approached the hundredth anniversary
of that event

I remain in awe
remembering
how we quivered in our desks
thirty obedient students
wondering what to believe

After Math

every year since graduation
has been something
of an aftermath
with the memory of when
Mrs. Carter
stood alone at the blackboard
ruling the chalk line
with little cardiogram blips
of white residue
notched into the woody
equidistance like the measure
of music
in birdsong
as by the metronome
of her sweeping arm
she followed
the distance along
a slate-black wall
her voice muted by
the slab at the most
pedagogical end of the room
and it was of Newton
and Euclid and
Pythagoras we learned
by Mayan nullity and
Arab equations and in deference
to the golden mean
we walked in and sat down

in miniskirts and
go-go boots and
bellbottoms flaring
over the grey-black skuff
of Cuban-heel Wellingtons
or the suede buff
of snow-damaged desert boots

and the clock on the wall
twitched its lean hands
as though on an itch
with a sexual shift of time
in *everybody*
like the lassitude of adolescent ennui
wondering would she send
the last nubbin of chalk
soaring over her shoulder
like a stone-startled moment
in some farm boy's life
some hard on the head
reminder of where he was
and why he was there
lost in the dreamy swirl of dusty daylight
the mind of all
like a book clapped shut
on the word
and the heart
like the stumblebum drumming
of a dumb bird
a cardinal cock pecking a window
to punish

the rival reflection
of the other self
the one you once were
before the true self
told you that you weren't actually there
like most everyone else
simply counting the grain
for the gods of a golden field

Not Everyone Knows ...

"Ingenious, Miss Lee"
her history teacher
had said to my sister
puzzled by the wonder of it
those words
conjuring a possibility
she came home
curious to know
what he'd meant
when what he'd meant
was *a kindness*
as she confesses now
that she was always
bored in his class
and distracted
so when a question she only half heard
drifted her way
landing like a seed kite
feather-dusting her attention
hooking her mind
away from window dreaming
with an inquisitive itch
and she conjured a guess
a non sequitur
some fanciful disconnection
concerning the senate of Rome
he'd simply squinted
as was his half-blind habit

and said
"ingenious, Miss Lee"
leaving her to puzzle
even at the supper table
as winter evening soaked the glazein black
like an ink stain spilling over the house

"Does ingenious mean
he thinks I'm a genius?"

and what our mother thought
and what our father
thought, and what
our uncle thought
went all unsaid or
unremembered --

well as for me
I know he meant to do her *a kindness*

there's no answer
that's ever so wrong
it requires
a harsh correction

intelligence is a weapon best kept
careful of the heart

As You Will Recall

a tribute to my high-school history teacher Mr. She

he was a genuine scholar, true to the faith in all learning
eccentric and nearly blind
he stood at the front
of our class
affecting the pedagogical squint
of the absent-minded
clichéd idiosyncrasies of a man
of uncommon erudition
his grey suit
clipped at the ankles
so his trousers ballooned
over his calves in high-water fashion
like English jodhpurs
meant for safety in cycling
and his lapels
were chalky with residue
pollen-dust yellow
and butter-coloured at the cuff
from when he came over-close to the slate
careless of his sleeves
he'd smudge the ephemeral lessons
like the passing of weather
over the sun
as with a didactic blur
the time-doomed Hittites went the way
of all lost civilizations

and we were lettered
and the numbered
C3, D5, A4, E7 etc.
we stood to be called
into bicameral legislative
governance, confederates in the butternut
states of American knowledge
or plebeians and plutarchs
of ancient Rome like wine stains
in a linen tablecloth we remembered the past
we thought of the sad
ostracisms of Athenian hills, of the fires of
Alexandria, or the chimerical nonsense
of carpet bombing the immolated peasants
of Cambodia, or of the madness of Mai Lai

and what a strange
fascination I felt
thinking of my own mind
as that of a common concern
with a universal admiration
of that most singular man

until recently
when my sister said to me
he was so boring
she confessed of herself
as suffering the drowsy doldrums
of adolescent ennui -- to her
he was droning
his voice

like the wings of a swarming
of wasps cooling a hive in a wall
revealing
how different we were she and I
even then –

and every summer's end
when I returned to his class
the first phrase he uttered
"as you will recall ..."
as though
in both the Julian and in
the Augustinian heat
of those halcyon months
we'd been thinking of nothing
but the last words
he'd spoken on the last
unlasting days of June ... *remember this ...*
those words like a rope
he'd dropped down a well

when we were the water
and he was the sky

In the Evening of My Youth

in the autumn of '68
I turned seventeen
living life in the throes
of my most adolescent libido
under the awe
of the fifth vowel, suffering
unwanted tumescence
in the sexy ululation of words
libidinous verbs
and lascivious nouns
watching the walk-away
in the hem sway like soft bells
of the short-skirt girls

and yet it was also
a year of assassins
Bobby Kennedy's
broken skull cradled
in the upturned palms
of care-filled sorrow
in a hotel kitchen
in a clatter of California
his beautiful death
floating as in a sorrowful river of crimson
like chivalric ribbons of war
flowing away to the floor

and also
the hotel balcony in Memphis

overlooking a parking lot
a single rifle shot sharp in the mind
and he dropped
like the tired burden
of a good man's soul

and it was also
a summer of smoke
in the border town
an industrial burn
that blackened the sky
from across the water at Windsor
the homes of the poor
the ash-garden
of the motor city
drifting up from the river

and the Mai Lai of one American May
one long-ago innocent May ...
that lilac blooming month of May
to hear the bloody screams
that we heard from afar
in the massacred village of Vietnam
how might we then
run from ourselves
as though we were not chased by ourselves
oh the smoke-flowered muzzles of guns
oh the flames in root of the heart
leaping like weeds from the earth

and it was also
murders in L.A.

it was murders
in tinsel-town mansions
and madness in songs on the air

and it was
a suppertime
of Nixon in the White House
a suppertime of riots on TV

and in the evening of my youth
in the winter the snow
came down veiling
the light at the barn
like what you might see
in the glow of a ghost
or the breath of an angel
were you not sleeping the sleep of the young

Expertise

I hate how I feel
infantilized by gadgetry
one summer of necessity
we purchased a flip phone
the first, last, and only time it rang
I flipped it open with confidence
as with these blunt fingers, these farmer's hands
I started making
a film of the *fucking* floor
I watched on the cellphone screen
an image in miniature of myself
scanning my feet
like incompetent espionage
as though for the want
of subterfuge concerning footwear
as though I were a foreign spy
from the courts of Phillip of Spain
inquiring *dondeesta el zapataria?*
and there I stood
like a toddler wielding a pistol
I felt that dangerous

and I'm brought to remember
the day
my favourite history teacher
the one who spoke
several languages
the one

who could fascinate
a room full of adolescents
with a single photograph
of Myron's *discus thrower*
and by way of that sculpture
teach the entire history
of an ancient civilization
as we lingered for days in class
in contemplation of culture
as seen through the eyes
of an artist
and we never grew time tired
surrendering ourselves to the guidance
of a fine mind

yet--he gave in to those
who said he must of necessity
show us a movie
and so
when it was 'lights out'
the reel leapt to life
ejecting itself from the projector
the film unspooling
across the floor
racing down the aisle of desks
like a long-tailed cat
while the hot light of the lamp
burned through melting gel
and the image on the screen
swam like chemical fire
glimpsed through isinglass

and I saw
how his proud shoulders sagged
as though with age
and how his mouth
quivered downward at the corners
and his
sad eyes clicked and blinked
in the salt-smart of tears

and I felt so damned sorry
I wanted to say
I'd rather hear your voice
any day of the week
than that studied chatter
of the overtalker
reading from a prepared script

and I wanted
to tell him how
my maternal grandfather
had taught me

let the hammer do the hammering
always spit on the nails
then drive them home
in the wood

and I saw in the sap weep how it was true

let the saw do the cutting
don't work so hard
see how the teeth are set

for ease just draw it like a knife
don't push, the weight of the saw
is all you need

and I looked along the line
of the metal
and saw how like a shark's jaw
the teeth leaned
left and right left and right
all the way from handle to toe

I wanted to say
… *it's never the tool*
it's always the man

see how the wall rises
into the rafters
like a great ship buoyed by water

give me a gift for the doing
and the spirit
of something I'll build
going backwards to first fire
with the shaman's voice in the dark

Old Chestnuts

I was a child of the sixties
when the elders
kowtowed to the callow wisdom of youth
and the pedagogues
lost their most serious minds
to the tyranny of teenage opinion

oh poor Thomas Hardy
toiling in candlelit Wessex
went wasting away on the shelf
a hundred copies
of the same old drudge flickering
gone stale on the pages
with rain on dry earth
like water in ink

and the weed-wild heart
of an untended garden
went war-dry and iron-red
with the blood of dead strangers
that weather — a suffering sky
where the plough-pullers plod
in a casual doom of lost days

what the bright bands sing
while new foil shakes
in the black fascination
of the crow beak of boys

while in the papers of the day
radishes leapt to the light
for want of the sound of Lennon's guitar

and American soldiers
seeded the flesh of a far-away village
with crimson welts
like rice in the soul of the field

how then might Hardy
speak to me revivified in tired lines

"Thou suffering thing
Know that thy sorrow is my ecstasy
That thy love's loss is my hate's profiting."★

here in the mind of a child
where old chestnuts fall
there's fertile earth enough in youth
for ancient shades to cool the light
with new leaf every spring

★lines from Thomas Hardy's poem "Hap," 1866

Himmelstoss in High School

as I walk my dog
between these rows
of man-planted maple saplings
their sharp-limbed shade
knifing into the earth
like seams of shale
I am reminded
of the ugly symmetry
of compulsory cadets
when I was an adolescent soldier
standing at ease
on the inner-track parade ground
at school
just after dropping my arm
in a right-dress shuffle
first affecting the rigid attention
of painted wood
then after much
sergeant-major barking
to be given permission
to relax
into the posture
of a laundry peg
legs akimbo, eyes front, no smiling
however self-amused
and then the itch set in
for we were wearing
army-surplus woolens

short brass-button jackets
and stove-legged trousers
held at the waist
by policeman's braces
with a tamoshanter
tucked under the left shoulder epaulet
or worn at a cock on the head
the brim two-fingers above the eyebrow
the badge of regiment on full display

and for petty martinet
the enthusiastic senior
would come
screaming along the line
watching for the odd smirk
of a smart aleck
or the nervous twitch
of a skittish lad

and to say
I hated the human cost
of blind obedience
some dutiful types
wilting with enthusiasm
fainting on their feet in stiff compliance
and falling flat as a trundle bed
face down in the dirt

to say "I hated being there"
would be
to understate my antipathy

for that military rectitude
that *befehlistbefehl*
end-of-school-day
when we gathered
into those *yes-sir* ranks
trimming the wick
as we wheeled-- and where
wonderful sloven Toad H. inquired
of the panjandrum on parade
"but sir, what if
my balls are itchy?"

and that broke the rank
like a farm deferment

there is no cure for the class clown
as he reaches for his crotch
grinning at rage
like the first of us all born to die laughing

Sadie Hawkins Dance, RDHS November, 1969

Sadie Hawkins was a character in the comic strip Li'lAbner. According to the tradition created in that strip, there was one day in the calendar year when the girl might pursue to object of her attention. In the case of the dance in question, it was a high school dance where girls were encouraged to ask a boy to the school dance.

now she would be
an old woman
as I am an old man
but that day
she walked up to me
in the hall between classes
accompanied as she was
by a girlfriend
for what one might call
moral support
with the shy-bold importuning
of that turnabout
moment when a girl
might ask a boy to a dance
and how could she
or her gleeful companion
have known
how shy I was
how fearful my longing
how often
stunned into silence

I felt
in the presence
of *girls*
like a sleepwalker
startled awake
like someone caught in a lie
or a thief
in the pantry at midnight

and I said 'yes' accidental
and sent them away
giggling behind their hands
and giddy
as though I were famous
as though
I had sprinkled stardust
on their shoulders

all day I agonized
thinking 'what to do, what
to do … oh, dear me, what to do'
how to go back on my word
how to
let her down gently
how to lift myself
out of the well
that echo chamber of my soul

and so
cap in hand

I found them –
walked up and withdrew
my 'yes' with the thread of a lie
for a hook 'my father won't let me
have the car'

even to my ears
it seemed lame

and the girlfriend
stepped forward
and slapped me down
with the heavy gauntlet
of her indignation
scorning me with epithets
and euphemistic curses

and so when they left
they stomped away angry
shedding the stardust like dander
oh my brief celebrity
it was fixed as a sham
as though that magic were cinder
from my hand
like the smudge of cold fire and
dead ashes

an old man now
I look back
at the asking or the having been asked
that flattery of being
seen as worthy of wooing

and I wonder
if the girls
lost deep inside the lives
of the old women
both the one
giggling with glee
and the one
mortified by refusal
ever forgave me or
just for a moment
considered it was
the fear of disappointment
when I failed
to live up
to the promise of dancing

Sex Education

in my generation
there was mostly an adult silence
when it came
to matters of sex
my father said nothing
my mother
said less, and the teachers as schoolmarms
stood tapping their disapproving shoes
and so we were left on our own
to discover the world
of the body
like lambs at frolic
or calves at play
when the changes came
to an April crop
in August when the first naughty feelings
surged in slow fires
scorching the field
and sweeping the meadow in shade
the rams were brought in
to bleat at the edge of the pen
and the young bulls
were gathered to bellow together
corralled in a board-fenced yard
rubbing their shoulders on stone
while we were abandoned as children in trust
we boys with our centerfold fantasies
and girls with red-ribbon

gifts from the moon
how to reconcile then
the romantic thrill of a sweet stolen kiss
and innocent blushes
from brushing of thighs in a dance

or the rustle of taffeta
and the feel of a three-cloth breast
where the heart drums through
bent bone like red thunder
in the pulse points of the mind
tracing a fuse
like pulling a thread
to its source in the fabric of flesh
come loose from the spool of all things

and so
in co-ed at seventeen
we were considered
as ready for truth
and Mr. McCarty
gathered us in a class
to warn us all of the need for a care
especially the girls
for whom there was only
the prospect of pain
and the agony of disappointed desire

what awaits them
is the loss and then
the stigma of shame

while boys for pleasure
dream of something that doesn't exist

we studied girls
who died for love like Juliet
and drowned Ophelia
all fallen women locked away
in books like words we dare not use

The Boy in the Broken Mask

I'd been told often enough
when I was quite young that I was cute
and I almost began to believe it
seeing my face
in the oval bedside mirror
the one pretending to be me
sometimes seemed to confirm
that he was indeed
his mother's son
for she was movie-star stunning
Grace Kelly lovely
like the girl in the woods
the one the evil queen hated
so much for her pulchritude
she poisoned her rival
with a red apple that put her to sleep
awaiting the gaze and the lingering kiss
that would wake her from dreaming

I remember the second glances
with girls
giggling behind their hands
as they passed me in the high school hallway
one of whom
told my sister
that if I weren't so weird
all the girls would be after me
and so I confess

I sought out the looking glass
lothario -- the one
the girls saw
and there he was
in the rearview mirror
there he lurked
in silver reflection
there he saw himself seeing himself
on the staircase at Hudsons
coming down with the Beatles *Revolver*
tucked under his arm
no -- you're not the one
they see
you cannot be the one
you surely aren't he
and that isn't me
that can't be me
walking to shore
in the lake at Rockport
splashed by the flirtatious fanning of water
breezing up from the hand of a beautiful stranger
nor are you, nor ever were you
not ever the boy on the bale
at London Fair
sitting next to the city girl
who sidled so close
you felt the heat of her hip
on your own ...

and so, not quite believing the evidence
you took your first camera

the *Brownie Starmite*
and you snapped a shot or yourself
with a hot sizzle of brilliant light burning
to confirm to yourself
it was you in the eyes of the others
but when the film came back from the drugstore
and you ruffled the deck
for that image
there it was
and there you were
with your face in the pack
two dark nostrils
poked in your father's long nose

startled Narcissus
and the laughing joker sorrowing
up from the floor
the jangle of his cap
like bells in a bird cage
and the boy hiding
behind the wall
the one in the broken mask
disguised as himself till then

I Can't Believe it Myself Most Days

I can't believe it myself most days ...

"Teachers must no longer be the sage on the stage.
Now we must become the guide by the side." She intoned.

"What about the goof
on the roof?" He inquired.

(An exchange between a pedagogue seeing herself as bringing the
tablets down from the mountain, and a mischief-maker at the
end of a presentation during a secondary school staff meeting.)

The last time I saw my grade eight teacher Miss Myrtle Downie,
former principal of SS No 12, the three-room elementary school I
attended in the village of Highgate, I had already been a secondary
school teacher of English, Dramatic Arts, and Creative Writing at
a six-hundred pupil rural school in Waterford, Ontario for almost
a decade. I hadn't seen her since graduation day in 1965 when I
was a callow lad on the cusp of thirteen, and she was an ancient
lady most likely in her late forties or early fifties. Now she lived
in the same retirement residence as my maternal grandmother.
I was very glad to see her. I had apologies to make. She smiled at
me from the comfort of her small room, looked me hard in the
eye and said, "John, you look so natural."

I had grown my hair long as soon as I left the farm. My
hair had begun to curl when puberty struck and by the time

I started university I quit using hair tonics to tame my tresses and let my 'freak flag fly'. One of my great heroes was the famous electric guitar virtuoso and force of nature, Jimi Hendrix. I'd far rather have had hair like Paul McCartney, but that just wasn't the coiffure for me with my wild doo. I let it grow and fate decided my natural curl would morph into an Afro. If I tell people now, "I once had an Afro that would fill a doorway," they look at me with disbelief and laugh to imagine. Little wonder matronly Myrtle Downie would be so open with an offhand compliment. Or so I took it. "You look so natural," she'd said smiling. And I'd thanked her for that. She continued briefly, holding my gaze with hers, "I never thought that you, of all people, would ever become a teacher. I thought you hated teachers." And I realized as she said this, that she meant that she had thought I hated teachers in general and her in particular. I suppose the evidence of my conduct as a very immature and slightly smart alecky pipsqueak, a bespectacled Poindexter of slight stature, unathletic, feckless, and sickly with an unruly lickspittle cowlick sproinging out of my crown like a busted spring on a head-sized clock must have suggested an antipathy for pedagogues.

To tell the truth I didn't hate teachers and I certainly never held her in contempt. I do remember one particular day when I was showing off for the girls, trying to get a laugh during story time. Ironically, I loved story time. And if I recall correctly, the story teacher was reading from that day was *The Jungle Book*, by Rudyard Kipling. Every school day following afternoon recess Miss Downie would read to us for fifteen minutes or so. And I loved those sessions. Being read to from a classic is one of my elementary school favourite recollections. And Kipling's novel was something of an apotheosis from those halcyon occasions.

That said, my good friend Gerald Grant and I would often compete with one another showing off and trying to get the other to laugh and maybe even descend into fits of giggles. I suppose I must have been pulling faces, and whispering silly things, juking and engaging in general hijinks all without gaining the attention of teacher who was reading to us from the front of the room. Miss Downie finally had had enough of me. I had failed to remain sufficiently intrepid. She snapped shut her book and stamped her foot like an angry ewe warning I'd come too close to the lamb. She called my name and pointed over her shoulder to the door at the front of the classroom leading into the small bookroom where all who went there knew the axiom *'Abandon hope all ye who enter here,'* for this instruction bore the consequence of a verdict. This was where you went to receive *the strap.*

I was of the 'spare the rod and spoil the child' generation. I had received the strap any number of times in the early years of my first instruction. My best friend in grade one Dicky Lewyll had received the strap so often the palms of his hands were weathered like old paint. And I had grown accustomed to the red sting often enough to avoid provoking the need. That day in grade eight would be the first occasion in many years that I would be found worthy of anything so Draconian. I obeyed Miss Downie. I walked tuck tailed and dutifully into the torture chamber. She pulled the door shut leaving me alone inside. "I'll be there in a minute," she said. And there I stood in that bookish silence surrounded by volumes I'd read and some I had not. I loved the school-bus yellow pile of *National Geographic,* the ones the eldest Roust boy used to read hard-swallowing a half-chewed wad of his fried-egg sandwich all the while thumbing the pages as he gulped. I can still almost smell the yolky fragrance of fried eggs and hard globs of country butter whenever I behold an uncut *Geographic.*

Time passed like the slow drip of a leaf tip in a light rain. Silence dried the air in that dry-aired room. The doorknob turned. The door creaked open. And Miss Myrtle Downie entered and closed the silence behind her. There we two were, cramped in that small room--I with my shame; she with her stern intent. And then she said simply, "You aren't a bad boy, Johnny. I'm sure you'll be better behaved in future. Let us never speak of this again."

I do not recall what I said. I only recall that for the first time in my life I realized that teachers were human. I realized that she suffered to think of giving the strap as much as I suffered to anticipate the hot sting of it being administered.

So that day years later in the retirement home when she'd said to me, "I thought you hated teachers," I wanted to throw my arms about her and to embrace her and to say, "No! I didn't hate teachers. I didn't even know that teachers were human. I used to think that when teachers left the school they went home and hung their bodies on wooden hangers like mothy overcoats, or tossed themselves in chairs like drop-stringed marionettes. Teachers didn't eat or sleep or play. In summer they estivated like woolens in a cedar trunk. I didn't hate teachers. And I certainly didn't hate you."

We sipped our tea that day as equals. I in my Afro and she in her faux pearls and teacher shoes with coffee mug heels, two teachers taking our ease. I didn't know it then, but I would defenestrate after only fourteen years in the classroom. Although I enjoyed my profession, I preferred writing to teaching and the opportunity to become a full-time writer presented itself in my life. And so, I jumped out the window and fled the profession in my early thirties.

Now, I'm sixty-four and since I left full-time teaching in the summer of 1990, I've had ample opportunity to keep my oar in the water. I've done workshops in writing from kindergarten through grade thirteen. I've taught neophytes barely beginning their alphabet and advanced writers with many books to their credit. I've lectured all over the world. I've taught literature at several universities and been the guest of English Departments from Maine to Wisconsin to Nelson Mandela's alma mater Witwatersrand in Johannesburg, South Africa. I've served as writer in residence at several universities and in several libraries. And I've learned a few things that I take to heart. *Never steal anyone's joy* is my major credo; and *better a bad poem than a good bomb* my Cri de Coeur.

★

Unlike me, my wife spent her entire working life as a teacher except for brief interruptions due to maternity leaves and the vicissitudes of ill health. I became a teacher of necessity. What else might an English major do? Although I would argue that she was far more naturally suited to becoming a great teacher than I, Cathy followed me into the profession the September after we were married. We came home from our honeymoon in late summer 1974, walked into the admissions office at Althouse College, and threw ourselves on the mercy of the administrator saying, "We'd like to go here." It was a Friday afternoon and classes began on the following Monday morning. I enrolled in English and Dramatic Arts, and she enrolled in Physical Education and Guidance. Eight months later, just short of graduation, we were hired at Waterford District High School, both of us in our areas of specialization. Two years later we had permanent contracts. I taught for fourteen years until I defenestrated in favour of becoming a full-time writer. Although I went on to life as a somewhat peripatetic instructor, it was Cathy whose career in teaching was varied and challenging.

After teaching secondary school for ten years, in 1984 she was seconded to the W. Ross MacDonald School for the Visually Impaired in Brantford where she taught for several years while acquiring her specialist in Blind Education. Then she was hired

by the Brantford Board of Education as a teacher of elementary
school students who were in trouble with the law. In the
meantime, she acquired her specialist in special education and
her specialist in primary education and thereby became qualified
to teach children with special needs and she spent the remainder
of her career in several schools in the city teaching students who
were identified. She came home with stories to tell and it was her
career that inspired me to coin the phrase "I can't believe myself
most days," to describe her experiences in the system.

She always treated her students with utmost respect and
kindness. She championed their immediate needs and was a
vigilant advocate on behalf of their long-term educational
prospects. Many, though not all of them, were from disadvantaged
homes. The worst winter of her career came as something of a
nadir that is so awful to consider it seems impossible to believe.
She was teaching in a school situated in a relatively affluent
suburban region of the city. You might imagine that her principal
would be sympathetic to the plight of her students since he was
on a committee founded to advocate on behalf of the poor.
This could not have been further from the truth.

The poverty level of her students was such that several of them
did not own winter coats, boots, hats, or mittens. One poor lad
did not even own a pair of socks. In the fall she had been assigned
a classroom in a portable outside the boundaries of the school
building. She would often arrive to find one of her students there,
seated on the steps, shivering in a thin jacket, waiting for her to
open her door. Just before Christmas vacation, one of the parent
volunteers who worked at Wal-Mart as a manager convinced the
store to donate clothing for her students. She gave them each a
toque, mittens, a scarf and two pair of socks, along with candy
and a toy. The boys and girls gobbled up the candy, paid brief
attention to the toy, but they were absolutely thrilled by the

winter clothing. For some of them it would be the first mittens they had ever owned.

After Christmas vacation the students arrived in the portable to discover that the heating system had broken down over the holiday. When Cathy brought this to the attention of the principal, she was told to tough it out until the problem was solved. The temperature plunged and when it became unbearable to stay put, she brought her students into the school library where she set up class. The principal found out and told her to go back to the portable where her class belonged. They sat in the portable like orphans in the gulags of the Soviet, keeping warm by wearing winter apparel all day. When she approached her union representative to advocate on her behalf, she was told to follow orders. When she wrote a letter to the health and safety commission, the letter was intercepted and she was warned that if she persisted in her efforts she would be *written up* for insubordination and a letter would be put on file as the first step in the process toward dismissal. She had no recourse but to suffer, and to allow her students to suffer on for the entire month of January waiting for the janitorial staff to repair the heating system. This may seem so Dickensian as to make it sound like something right out of a nineteenth century novel. But this was the decade of Mike Harris when war was being waged on the poor. Little wonder I coined the phrase *I can't believe it myself most days*. Even as I write this I find myself thinking "Surely I'm exaggerating. Surely this cannot be true." Had I not witnessed it myself, I might be skeptical.

During her stint in the next school, a core city school with nothing like the resources that were available in middleclass regions of the city, she experienced deprivations on a school-wide basis that did not occur in her previous school. When the student washrooms ran out of soap and paper towel, the bathrooms went without being stocked for the remainder of the term. When the classrooms supplies were used up, they were not replenished. The Parents' Council in poorer neighbourhoods was able to make only very modest amounts of money through fundraising. One scheme involved a breakfast program for students. The food was donated by charity, the staff cooked the breakfast, and each student was asked to sign up for the program that cost twenty-five cents a week. When Cathy collected the money from her students she noticed that one of her most deserving children had not signed up for the breakfast. "Jimmy," she said. "You should sign up for this breakfast." "I can't Miss," he said. "And why not?" She inquired. "My mom doesn't have twenty-five cents, Miss."

That very morning I had heard a man interviewed on the radio saying he always sends his Versace socks to the dry cleaners. Versace Medusa Men's Navy-Gold Dress Socks retail at $26.99 American a pair. Only the day before a Russian oil tycoon had spent $52,000 on lunch at a posh restaurant in Manhattan. Is it little wonder I write *I can't believe it myself most days?*

But I do believe it. I believe it because it is true. I believe because it happened in my city in my lifetime on my watch within my experience as a teacher in a system that claims to be one of the best in the world. I always said of myself that I would create an oasis of excellence in my classroom. However pretentious that may sound, I dedicated myself to that ideal. Whatever else was going on in the world, whatever else went on outside my door, I would create an environment where children were safe and where together we might manage to take seriously the business at hand. I know that children suffer. Growing up is hard enough work. The best teachers are amongst the greatest champions of youth. And I have known some of the best teachers. Miss Myrtle Downie who came into our grade seven classroom to tell us that President John F. Kennedy had been shot gave us that news with a quavering voice because she cared profoundly about our young lives and she knew that we needed the reassurance that we are all in the same boat. Even in this 'I can't believe it myself most days' world, we are not alone. We are in the company of great teachers whose compassionate guidance we might feel even in our own later years. I can believe, and I do believe in a better world, an oasis of excellence, a place we might share even if only in a dream.

No Time for Lies

Ode to Librarians – a cynic's appraisal of these times

... if I were to say to you
most librarians don't read
would you become angry
indignant, outraged by
the unearned hubris
accuse me of being
orgulous – oh do we not
now live in an
anti–intellectual age
are we not steeped
in a stupefying culture where learning
is a sin of commission
where there is an insufficiency
of baskets – a scarcity
of sheltering shade
where intelligence might hide and
erudition lock up its light
in shadow like ginseng in sunlight while like rat moles
moiling in darkness
we blink at the brilliance
where all the Google-knowing
and all the fact-shaming rule
and all the conversational competition
in the COVID lonesome era
of the information age ...
why, there's even a service
for the quick know-nothings
who leap to their feet

with a know-it-all answer
a short-cut acquaintance
with no need to consider or comprehend
what is pi? What is the speed of light?
How many toes on a six-toed cat?

as you jump to your feet
with a cell-phone solution
you might easily own the floor
like a mouse in the moonlight
or a scurry of roaches
in a world where dancers can't dance
and singers can't sing
and poets who
though they've read nothing and
know less
hold forth from the stage
in the borrowed glint
of popular thought and clichéd phrases
but oh, how sincere, oh how 'woke' in a gender ambiguous age

and so I return
to my unopened book
and I ask of the dog at the door
or the dog on the step
what page are you on
and I look to his ear bent up and then down
for enlightenment
as he cocks his sweet head
for a selfie
and as I return the text to the shelf

from here I can see
how the librarian smiles
to think of it there
exactly where it belongs at rest in an organized heap

though the marginalia screams
like a gut-shot prayer

and the dying by which we die slowly
succeeds in hiding all that we know
from those that don't know it who think
that we wish we were them

Manuel in the Mush Hole

we were given a tour
of the now-closed Mohawk Institute
my Cuban friend
Manuel and I
following the rote recitation
of the trained guide
as we passed
from empty room to empty room
walking the echo-voiced
vacancy of the hallway
listening to our own
footfalls in the sleepy
book-drop of her studied incantation
passing from there through to the gruel-ghost
of the kitchen
where oat-wormed
porridge once boiled
in the served-cold steel
of a blue-pot morning
vermin veiled in the bitter breath of her words

and he tried to tell her
how it was exactly thus
for him
a rural lad in Castro's Cuba
stolen by learning
taken away from his father's
rope-ribbed horses

gone to where he lived
miles from home
the oatmeal breakfast
the same, the
lonesome scholar, the
same, the orphan's
depravation, the same
the homesick child, the
same, the cruel
isolation, the same
however
now Professor Léon
cannot gain her attention

wanting to tell her
how like a hothouse orchid
he felt the loss of the forest floor
forced as he was in painted light
as with each brushstroke
of the revolution
his past had faded
as a dream will fade in the day

on the back of an old photograph
guilty of having taught there
in the mush hole of 1907
my grandmother
has recorded the names
of every student
written in black relief of blunt graphite
as though those names

were an accusation
too cruel for smiling eyes of the girls
grown anonymous in imaginary sunlight
where a white dog lay on the lawn

Oh dear, oh my ...

when we dropped our elder son
off at student residence
so long ago in first year
a cabal of adolescent strangers
received his psyche
taking his hand as though
it were any old *we'll take it from here*
moment as we watched him
disappearing into
an open-door room
wondering what dwelt within
walking him past
a beer-bottle gauntlet
that stale familiar fragrance
of spilled fermentation
fluting the air
like the atomizing of a drunkard's sweat
and this was where
the living of one life stops and
where the other starts
entering as he was the final lustrum
of a learner's last decade
someone saying 'surrender your son
to the saturnalia
give him up
to these sacrificial years
to the illusion
of illumination'

like a light left on
in a vacant room
or the darkness
in a cave of bones

oh how we worried once
in a Fascist world
oh how we lived in fear
of Oppenheimer's
bomb, oh how
the dominos tipped
and nations fell to war
to war we went
oh the oceans rose
and the cities fell
and the wildfires
burned and great winds blew
and the desperate
diaspora swelled the borders
as children washed and their bodies rolled
like jetsam on the shores of paradise

oh dear, oh my ...
the same, the same
we see a cliff too steep to climb
we build a set of stairs
we fear a flood we
seek a higher ground

all future quarrels
wait like weapons in a drawer

the knife's a thief of time
it steals
the meaning from the past
and lingers in dried blood
remembering death
the ghostly whispers
of its warning breaths all rust away
until the sand within the iron
blackens earth become ferruginous red
and we are drawn
like magnets into filaments and files
that stand like hairs upon a frightened arm

When You're Slapped, You'll Take It and Like It

The morning after
the airing of *Gone with the Wind*
on commercial TV in the late 1980s
one of my grade nine students
raised her hand and asked
"Mr. Lee, did people really
used to think
that Clark Gable was handsome?"
and I could
tell by the tone in her voice
that she couldn't imagine
it was ever so
how explain to her
that the man
who suffered smoker's halitosis
whose kiss
was the taste of an ashtray
grinning and leaning in
for a close-up
his elbow resting
on the balustrade
made women of my mother's generation
melt like summer butter

and oh how they fell
like girls
in a swoon
on a fainting couch

at the sexy two-nostril
exhalation
of the man on the screen
like waving the veils
or walking through webs
or the sensuous fading of fog
that prickles the flesh
with an ephemeral grey caress
of nearly visible words
taking their time to expire

and when I confirmed
his status
as a lothario of a generation
disbelief
knocked my hat in the dirt

and I was not
wearing a hat
though my feet shivered
into the floor
with a stain on the ceiling below
like the rain you might walk
with the shadow of rain
going dry

James Reaney's Elbows

when the wise professor
leaned on the podium
waxing eloquent his soft voice quivering
on a fine literary feature
of an important text
his delicate hand raised
sawing the air
in a sort of academic karate
in service of some salient point
in the grip
of intellectual erudition
conducting the caesura
of a mot juste moment
a lacuna in the melody
a euphonious and lovely break
in refined language … all she noticed
was the frowsy garment
the trip-trouser cuff
the out-at-the-elbows
half-buttoned cardigan
he wore loose like a sheep-proud shepherd
the threadbare thing
*êtremiteux*as the French
might say
of the hill fighter
the maquis
hiding in the grotto
eating ripe cheese and stale bread

dipped in stolen wine
his fingernails earth-black
fire-black and bitten
to the scorch ...

how might we learn
from brilliant minds
when all we notice
is the distraction
Northrop Frye -- one step forward,
one step back one step forward
one step back (and repeat)
as though he were tethered to the rostrum
or Harold Bloom
late in life noshing every word
like a dry-mouthed drug
and how might we listen then
to Noam Chomsky
his wild hair flying in thin white wisps
like an old dandelion gone to seed
that white little Einstein of the wind
once lovely yellow in the green lawn of April
and my friend complains
of the ugly woman
chosen as spokesperson
how he cannot pay attention
how he longs for a Kokanee girl
with long tanned legs and firm breasts

let her speak, he might be shouting
she has something to say

JOHN B. LEE

Don't Smile Before Christmas

my late friend Jamie
the bookseller become
taxi driver
said to me -- John,
it's everything I can do
to not to come
to hate the poor --
and he wept in his bed
at the end of his life
for want
of leaving behind him
a better world
for his having lived
and we buried his beard
and his smiling eyes
in the soul-blind earth
under the healing grass
sealing over
the green wound
of his grave
so the sky could not find him
not the sun in the day, nor the stars
in the night, nor the moonlight that shone
on the bay while we dreamed
and were dreaming like snow on a stone

and I am brought to remember
Claudia -- the beautiful

bright-eyed young teacher
gone mad in the heartless crowd
of a cruel class of farm kids
a rural school in muskrat country

how they
wild-packed her weakness
like a meaningless kill
with none of them hungry
but for her blood
white as chalk she might leave on a wall

it's everything I can do
to not to come
to hate the poor

he'd said
listening to Yo-Yo Ma

while he waits for a fare
as he waits
for want of a better world

JOHN B. LEE

From the Outside Going In

the man who is the brother
to the man we know
is giving us a lesson
on how to form
an origami grasshopper
from thumb-broad blades
of Cuban palm fronds
he is an expert
of this folk art
he learned it in his youth
and now
we tourists are
his humble students
one of our number
is such a quick study
it's as though
she were born at the feet
of the master
achieving the knots of the thorax
the bend of the legs
the what-to-us
has become complicated plication
like the linen flowers
appearing on our bed sheets in the morning
the maid's abandoned peonies
blessing us as though
blossoms had fallen from the improbable
garden of their hands

and this fellow traveller
cannot resist
coming to us each and all
and she is most frustrated with me
for I have fashioned
a whip-tailed monster
a green tease
a scorpion gone but for his sting
oh, I've a spider
on a stick
I've a hissing serpent
I've a feather-tipped sword
I've a nest of knots
meant only for the minty squeeze
and I'm left
picking my teeth like a yokel with hay
the one and only true artist
the sculptor in our midst
is the most surprised
by his own ineptitude
for he thought he'd be first-in-class
though he looks to his own result
and sees
something broken
like a born-wrong beetle
a green scribble of weed
something so hand-blind
it became a fracture in the cradle of creation
something like an open egg
that fell too far

but the aforementioned woman
the instant expert of origami grasshoppers
insists herself into every attempt
but for mine ...
me she sees as helpless
hopeless, a waste of her precious time
though only the teacher and I
see in the glorious machinery of her every movement
the true reason she burns to be best
and it consumes her from the outside
going in

Stupid Boy

at the end of my adolescence
I came home to the farm
from my freshman year away from home
my mind broken
by the profligate and self-destroying
life of a wastrel child
and my greatest fear
-- the fear of night
where even the sheep were strange
and I became
a shepherd of meaningless madness
a leaping into the fence uncountable past one
frantic beast head-caught in wire
where midnight darkness
came pouring down the window glass
blackstrap slow
and sickly sweet
as heaven like a coal face blind as stone
slipped through the shining glaze
and gave my little room
a shadow veil of demon gauze
that fell upon my form and
smouldered off the floor
like watered smoke

though I was but a briefly damaged boy
I might have channeled Lear

O let me not be mad, not mad
Sweet heavens, keep me in temper
I would not be mad

and there I lay
a lonesome occupant of solitary night
a dreamer fearing sleep become
a sleeper fearing dream

and what to do
but live within that awful cave
of absent light
alone alonealone
cold summer of the dimming soul
the brain
inside the flesh
unstoppered like a waving cork
above an open bottle mouth
resealed, reveals
the synesthesia of the terrifying taste of time

the black hand of morning reaching through
the brilliant darkness of
another dawn

I lost a year of youth
and having lost a year
regained the next in finding love

Why is it That Girls Love Screaming

for Tai Grove after reading P.K. Page's poem "Little Girls"

he listens
to the voices
rising through the air coming up and out and
over the schoolyard in the distance
and he wonders
why is it
that girls love screaming
he hears the shrill siren
of their glee
lifting like the caterwaul
of seagulls
competing for space on the sand
where they've landed
like shipwrecked angels
and no peacock stranger
fanning its blind-eyed tail
could be more beautifully
and zoologically odd
in a quiet neighbourhood
than these
wild children declaring
themselves
no alone-on-an-island
keening at the blue indifference
of an empty sea
could seem more meaningless

in its roaring
to the vacant horizon
beyond the syllables of a hopeless importuning

what the wind can't drown
it carries
aloft like leaves
and the full-sail scraps
of sound
as unremembered and unremembering
vocables that simply *shrill* and *howl*
and go to the ghost of bottle flutes
and window sills
that haunt the very storm dogs
of the adult mind

Ode on a Photograph of six Mohawk Schoolgirls circa 1906

all of those beautiful
adolescent Mohawk schoolgirls
immured in permanent
imagination of a sepia tone
photograph
preserved by my paternal
grandmother's
pedagogical gaze
when she too was a virgin
in the vestal innocence
of her modest youth
their beatific faces
glowing in their pinstripe gowns
their black hair shining
beribboned and comb-caught
the delicate lace ruff
of their collars
foaming out like filigreed snow
one fastened by a single pearl button
the others
nun-drab and hasped
from within
they lapse into time
like the falling outward
into the light
of the vaporous drifting away
of mist over water

what is clarifying blue
to them moves
the pen within my hand
for all that remains
of the half-seen arc
at the crest of a chair
and the decorative backdrop
of a photosensitive wall
the shop in the city
breaking its red-heart bargain
with these girls
for whom life in the light
is long over
though for them
in that moment
it was *everything*

Listening to a Schoolgirl Reading a Pauline Johnson Poem During a Dedication Ceremony in the Poet's Garden at Port Dover as I Hold a Six-Thousand-Year Old Flint Arrowhead in my Hand

we were planting Echinacea
with a thought for Pauline
her poetry read by a girl
vanishing into the breath
of the wind
as our words are sometimes
subsumed in the voice of large weather
and lost in the voluminous
rattle of leaves
that nearly perfect
ensouling of language
like seeing
the ghost of old ink
coming dark through the page
of a book
a reversal of font
or the hint of pressing gone dry
in the blot

and what did I hold in my hand
as I listened
what whispered away in my palm
from the Holocene age
on the cusp of the bronze
come late when the plough

turned the mind of the earth
to measure the field fence to fence
and the well fell to cups
and the woodland gave way
to blown sand

it was sharp
as the cruel light of morning
come piercing
the dreamer in sleep
oh Chonnonton fletcher
I feel how your spirit comes notched
in the lines of my flesh
as the singing to silence
gives way
at the end of a prayer
or a song

I Don't Remember the Moonlight but I Do Remember the River

I don't remember the moonlight
but I do remember the river
as I sat
in the grey-water darkness
of an autumn evening
in early October of my youth
there on the dreary banks of the Thames
at the edge of an audible flowing
feeling only mostly the emptiness of life
in the cruel-to-the-lonesome
middle of the Forest City
and what I wanted
was merely to vanish
like smoke blown thin over a burning landscape
as in a departiculation of despair
I rattled the ashes
in a small pink box of pills
given me by Dr. Oblivion
in a dreamless wash of nothingness
the day before morning
loveless and unloving
I had become lost in the blank sadness
of a sorrowless mind
well beyond woeful
wishing more to never have been - more
this than to cease to exist
to be unfound and forever unfindable

no stone-eyed god in his garden
no sinning by hands or by heart
in that diffident darkness
no miss-me scent clothing hung in the closets of home
if I consider
a moment's deciding
by the fluvial silt of that time-measured water
come clear in a settling rain
to die like a book in the mind of its author
lined pages all tearless and white
at the dropping of lead from his hand

An Important Failure

for me first year university French
was a classical disaster of epic proportion
I'd missed almost every class
did not attend the labs
dabbled in debauch
and the farouche life of a wastrel
leading to this debacle
seeing the tragic poet and the bucolic lad
the Byronic hero
come home swimming the Hellespont
like a moon-dumb dog and then …

the news of my failure came in the mail

how low I'd set the bar for mediocrity
a limbo measure for the nascent mind
slinking under
the fences like the light in a midnight puddle
to where my father was there, waiting
with a word for his son
who was sure to amount to *nothing*

and that was my most important failure
I fell like an apple-hearted orchard
blooming in April come to cider by autumn

yet I resolved to be glorious
and I gave myself this project

read more, read deeper, dive in
visit again, and then rerevisit
the past in the present
see how memory works its magic
how what we miss in dreaming is *everything*
sometimes more than everything
this *nothing* as lifting off the earth
like a shadow of let loose branches
I leapt

The Guitar Lesson

there is a painting
from the 1930s
by Balthus
so controversial, so outrageous
that it was hung
in a secret room
for the private viewing
only of a select few

were I to describe it here
it would surely light a fire
in the mind
as dark as basalt
burning in the bowels
of the earth

and I have been told
by friends
such stories
of music teachers
with twelve inch rulers
hovering over the hands
of children
like the sword of Damocles

those crack knuckle moments
that come
when boys and girls fail to arch their fingers

as they are meant to go spidering over the ivories
like lady harpists of a delicate web

who reads the silk
when the fly is like an angel
caught within a net of heaven

as the fisherman says
only the slow, or the stupid or the greedy
surrender to the snare

What Happened to You

we were talking over beer
comparing our experience
as children of the early sixties
the decade of the Beatles
and the summer of love
when half naked girls
danced in the mud at Woodstock
with a garland of flowers in their hair
a delicate crown of nature
like maidens of the maypole
their sun-stained bodies
the dreamed of lovers we'd
have taken in our arms in the garden
of the peaceable kingdom waltzing like misty nimbus
of light and fire-lit smoke
in a swirl of fabric
of forests in hazy linen
draping the branches like Spanish moss

but this was real
and we were true to our memory
of being in grade three
when failing a test in class
meant the need of a parent's signature
and Roger confessed that he'd lost
his paper on the way home
so the next day the teacher
called him to the front of the room

where he extended his hand palm to ceiling
as punishment for the crime of being a negligent boy
and he said of his pedagogue
that she has mastered a technique
for lashing the hand so the strap struck
not only the lifeline, not only the small bones of the fingers
but it also caught the delicate pulse point
just above the meat of the palm just below the cuff button
where the shirt sometimes frayed from labour
where the blue veins could be seen
in a translucent network leading to the heart

and then again the next day
and then again the next
for he dare not tell his father
for fear of getting worse at home

and the final occasion of the last of the strapping
she broke the blistered flesh
so it bled
and in the evening of the fourth day
he could no longer conceal
the obvious hurt
and his father inquired of him
concerning that stigmata of the schoolroom

what happened to you

and he quivered to confess
but his father
who was a hard man

a French Canadian lumberjack by trade
wept for his son

and this, dear reader
was what it was like for us

we who suffered
the truth of our times
hiding our wounds from
losing our failures
when home isn't waiting
like broth and unguent
and the healing ointment of mother's kisses

we who dreamed
the dreams that children dream

JOHN B. LEE

The Lonesome Blast Furnace of the Solitary Heart

was it *education* or
indoctrination
or *assimilation*
that brought a silent and
obedient subservience to bear in the
taming of the feral child
so that rather than racing
indoors breathless
with wonder, we lined up
in quiet queues, standing still
under the sign on the boy's door
over which
our gender blazed in lettering
chiseled into the masonry
of the cement lintels like identified death
and we answered to the
bell call
like the big weather booming
of the clangor that brings the cattle in
from the dark field
we filed in wagging the links of our chains
like beads on an abacus -- pausing
at first to slake a seemingly unslakeable thirst
for we were fever warm
and grass lashed
and graveling up at
the fountain, that slow-to-rise
font of the school well for want of the shining

of the low thread of silver water
and there we went
in tractable dutiful orderly fashion
to seat ourselves at our individual desks
which shrank as we grew
into leggy gangling
worshipful knee-knocks
we affected the posture
of crimped tin cramped and
bent in the middle being creased at the hip

our hands pressed palm up in prayer pose
work-callused fingers
nails bit to the quick
set by the inkwells that were hollow
as birdhouse doors
we were there in urgent stillness
catching the breath of the sound
come creaking out of the twinge in the floor
we almost quivered
with all the flesh could hold of the trapped-in energy
of nervous attentiveness

who dared to open a book
or drop a ruler
who sneezed or giggled
or worst of all *whispered*
or found himself watching a billet-doux slide
in a letter slot under the heel of a shoe
those sweet notes and
flirtations folded twice
and sometimes written in code

and after recess
as we blushed from the heat
of exertion outside
it was always 'story time'
in the punishing sentient drone
of teacher's voice
in the slow-death incuriosity
of the learning lustrum
of five-to-ten years in the chalk-dust
winters darkening down at ten to five
when the snow
rattled black glass
and seeped in at the sashes
and we learned about the white soul of ourselves turned grey
how the doors froze shut on the body
and something closed our eyes drowsy
with dreaming not a mortician's fingertips
but a lover's first kiss
setting old fires deep
within the lonesome blast furnace of the solitary heart

What Winters in Me is the Spring

we played chatterbox at school
that fortune teller origami
a whirlybird
of paper colours and numbers
and imaginary names
flashing in the hands
of a classmate – I also almost
believed in the possibility
of truth in playing cards
turned from the pack to the light
by my beloved aunt
amusing my cousins and me
on Sundays
her cheap bracelets
jangling like candy-coloured
moon rings
sliding elbow to hand
catching the motion
of her shuffling arm
settling like abacus
on the halo-nimbus knob of her wrist
seeing my future there
in a chance encounter
of knaves and aces
Queens and Kings and
with a two-hearted vision of whom I might meet
on the road leading away from tomorrow

and one night
we played Ouija
feeling the small delicate legged
planchette slipping over the board
like the tilting of liquid spilling *this-way that-way*
our fingertips light as sparrow bone
beware of the bad spellers
shivering over the alphabet
into the nether world
where ghost shadows shimmer and gutter
like dark winds in the oak shade of streetlamps

and now
I look back over life
more memory than dream
and even though
I remain full of wonder
recollecting the seasons
as seeds in an apple
climb to the drop-down of autumn
when the sheep on the farm
came rolling their jaws
on the windfalls
in the cider-stained grass
what winters in me
is the spring
and the sorrows that blossom

May the Torah Be Your Occupation★

the apple tree
outside my window
seducing the sky
with its fragrant and lovely allure
has opened its limbs to desire
from deep in the beauty of blossoms
in a brief and luxurious debauch
as over three minutes in May it calls

first the orange-breasted oriole
who arrives among flowers
thrusting his beak in each bloom
he sips at the font
with the delicate breeze
of his heaven held wings
his feathers aflame
at the resonant white
threshold of thrills
and as he departs
with a leap and a flash

the bumblebee
drones in with his basket
furred in the natural mindfulness of pollination
dabbing and buzzing and
buzzing and dabbing then
buzzing and rising away
like a sticky thumb stuck to a page

and *ah me* he is gone
and thence to dance a map
of the wind in the hive, meanwhile

the hummingbird
comes
his little wings
stitching the air in a blur as he's
quick to this
work with the thread of his tongue
he tickles an itch
as a loose thread will
when it strays on the flesh in a breeze

and now the blue-black iridescent feathered grackle
with a blink of his bright yellow eye
vanishes into the dark interior
where shadows are lost in the shade
and he rattles his body
and shatters the meaning of spring
so cascading petals litter the lawn
with a sad respond

I'm told
how the teachers of old
would slather with honey
the words from the scripture
written on slate
and the student
would lick the sweet language
as though in this

were to be found
the bee's intention
taking in the chalk and honey flavour
of those most holy of words

*these are the words from scripture written on slate by teachers who would slather the words with honey so the students, after reading the words aloud would lick the slate and thereby assimilate the words they were learning ...

Biographical Note

In 2005 John B. Lee was inducted as Poet Laureate of Brantford in perpetuity. The same year he received the distinction of being named Honourary Life Member of The Canadian Poetry Association and The Ontario Poetry Society. In 2007 he was made a member of the Chancellor's Circle of the President's Club of McMaster University and named first recipient of the Souwesto Award for his contribution to literature in his home region of southwestern Ontario and he was named winner of the inaugural Black Moss Press *Souwesto Award* for his contribution to the ethos of writing in Southwestern Ontario. In 2011 he was appointed Poet Laureate of Norfolk County (2011-14) and in 2015 Honourary Poet Laureate of Norfolk County for life and in 2017 he received a Canada 150 Medal from the Federal Government of Canada for "his outstanding contribution to literary development both at home and abroad." A recipient of over eighty prestigious international awards for his writing he is winner of the $10,000 CBC Literary Award for Poetry, the only two time recipient of the People's Poetry Award, and 2006 winner of the inaugural Souwesto Orison Writing Award (University of Windsor). In 2007 he was named winner of the Winston Collins Award for Best Canadian Poem, an award he won again in 2012. He has well-over seventy books published to date and is the editor of seven anthologies including two best-selling works: *That Sign of Perfection*: poems and stories on the game of hockey; and *Smaller*

Than God: words of spiritual longing. He co-edited a special issue of *Windsor Review—Alice Munro: A Souwesto Celebration* published in the fall of 2014. His work has appeared internationally in over 500 publications, and has been translated into French, Spanish, Korean and Chinese. He has read his work in nations all over the world including South Africa, France, Korea, Cuba, Canada and the United States. He has received letters of praise from Nelson Mandela, Desmond Tutu, Australian Poet, Les Murray, and Senator Romeo Dallaire. Called "the greatest living poet in English," by poet George Whipple, he lives in Port Dover, Ontario where he works as a full time author.

Books Published by John B. Lee

Poems Only A Dog Could Love, (poetry) Applegarth Follies, London, Ontario, 1976 88pp.

Love Among the Tombstones, (poetry) Dogwood Press, Simcoe, Ontario, 1980 80 pp.

Fossils of the Twentieth Century, (poetry) Vesta Publications, Cornwall, Ontario, 1983 75 pp.

Small Worlds, (poetry) Vesta Publications, Cornwall, Ontario, 1986 89 pp.

Hired Hands, (poetry and prose) Brick Books, 1986 85 pp.

Rediscovered Sheep, (poetry) Brick Books, 1987 80 pp.

★The Bad Philosophy of Good Cows, (poetry) Black Moss Press, Windsor, Ontario, 1989 77 pp.

The Hockey Player Sonnets, (poetry) Penumbra Press, 1991 85 pp.

★The Pig Dance Dreams, (poetry) Black Moss Press, 1991 91 pp.

When Shaving Seems Like Suicide, (poetry) Goose Lane Editions, Fredericton, NB, 1992 80 pp.

★The Art of Walking Backwards, (poetry) Black Moss Press, 1993 85 pp.

Variations on Herb, (poetry and prose) Brick Books, London, Ontario, 1993 95 pp.

All the Cats Are Gone, (poetry) Penumbra Press, 1993 77 pp.

★These Are the Days of Dogs and Horses, (poetry) Black Moss Press, 1994 81 pp.

Head Heart Hands Health: A History of 4H in Ontario, (non fiction) Comrie Productions, Peterborough, Ontario, 1994 224 pp.

★The Beatles Landed Laughing in New York, (poetry) Black Moss Press, 1995 79 pp.

★Tongues of the Children, (documentary poetry and prose) Black Moss Press, 1996 115 pp.

*Never Hand Me Anything if I am Walking or Standing, (poetry) Black Moss Press, 1997 91 pp.

*Soldier's Heart, (poetry) Black Moss Press, 1998 75 pp.

*Stella's Journey, (poetry and prose) Black Moss Press, 1999 85 pp.

*Don't Be So Persnickety, (children's verse) Black Moss Press, 2000 55 pp.

*Building Bicycles in the Dark: a practical guide to writing, (non fiction) Black Moss Press, 2001 135 pp.

*The Half-Way Tree: selected poems of John B. Lee, (poetry) Black Moss Press, 2001 150 pp.

In the Terrible Weather of Guns, (documentary poetry and prose) Mansfield Press, Toronto, 2002 97 pp.

The Hockey Player Sonnets: overtime edition (poetry) Penumbra Press, Ottawa, Ontario, 2003 98 pp.

*Totally Unused Heart, (poetry) Black Moss Press, 2003 66 pp.

*The Farm on the Hill He Calls Home, (memoir) Black Moss Press, 2004 155 pp.

*Poems for the Pornographer's Daughter, (poetry and prose) Black Moss Press, 2005 75 pp.

*Godspeed, (documentary poetry and prose) Black Moss Press, 2006 75 pp.

*Left Hand Horses: meditations on influence and the imagination, (essays) Black Moss Press, 2007 115 pp.

*The Place that We Keep After Leaving, (poetry) Black Moss Press, 2008 64 pp.

Island on the Wind-Breathed Edge of the Sea, (poetry) Hidden Brook Press, 2008 75 pp.

Being Human, (poetry) Sunbun Press, 2010 73 pp.

Dressed in Dead Uncles, (poetry) Black Moss Press, 2010 81 pp.

In the Muddy Shoes of Morning, (poetry) Hidden Brook Press, 2010 115 pp.

Sweet Cuba: Three-Hundred Years of Cuban poetry in Spanish and in English translation—John B. Lee and Manuel de Jesus (poetry and prose introduction) (Hidden Brook Press, 2010) 355 pp.

King Joe: A Matter of Treason—the life and times of Joseph Willcocks (1773-September 5, 1814) (popular history in prose) (Heronwood Enterprises, Summer, 2011) 85 pp.

Let Us Be Silent Here (poetry) (Sanbun Publishing, 2012) 85 pp.

You Can Always Eat the Dogs: the hockeyness of ordinary men (prose memoir) (Black Moss Press, 2012) 88 pp.

In This We Hear the Light (poetry and photographs) (Hidden Brook Press, 2013) 84 pp.

Burning My Father, (Black Moss Press, April 2014)

The Full Measure, (fall 2015)

Secret Second Language of the Heart, (Sanbun Publishing, spring, 2016)

The Widow's Land: superstition and farming—a madness of daughters, prose memoir, (forthcoming Black Moss Press, 2016)

This is How We See the World: the chapbook years, (Hidden Brook Press, 2017)

The Sesquicentennial Poems: Tai Grove and John B. Lee, (Sanbun Publishing, 2018)

Beautiful Stupid: selected and new 2001-2017 (Black Moss Press, 2018)

Into a Land of Strangers (Mosaic Press, 2018)

These are the Words: Bread Water Love George Elliott Clarke and John B. Lee, (Hidden Brook Press, 2018)

Into a Land of Strangers (Mosaic Press, 2019)

Moths That Drink the Tears of Sleeping Birds, (Black Moss Press, fall 2019)

Darling, may I touch your pinkletink, (Hidden Brook Press, 2020)

By &By:Small Pleasures, Don Gutteridge and John B. Lee, (Hidden Brook Press, 2020)

Flying on Wings of Poetry: Stronger In Broken Places, (one of four poets) (Hidden Brook Press, 2020)

The Heart Upon the Sleeve: Encomium, (one of four poets: two Cuban two Canadian) (Sandcrab publishing, 2021)

Something Else (Black Moss Press, 2021)

Chapbooks

To Kill a White Dog, (documentary poem) Brick Books, 1982 25 pp.

The Day Jane Fonda Came to Guelph, (poetry) The Ploughman Press, Whitby, Ontario, 1996 35 pp.

What's in a Name: the pursuit of George Peacock, Namesake of Peacock Point, (essay) Dogwood Press, Brantford, Ontario, 1996 15 pp.

In a Language with No Word For Horses, (documentary poems) above/ground press, Ottawa, Ontario, 1997 25 pp.

The Echo of Your Words Has Reached Me, (poetry) Mekler & Deahl, Hamilton, Ontario, 1998 20 pp.

An Almost Silent Drumming: the South Africa poems, (poetry) Cranberry Tree Press, Windsor, Ontario, 2001 33 pp.

Thirty-Three Thousand Shades of Green, (poetry) Leaf Press, Lantzville, BC, 2004 35 pp.

Though Their Joined Hearts Drummed Like Larks, (documentary poetry) Passion Among the Cacti Press, Kitchener, Ontario, 2004 22 pp.

Bright Red Apples of the Dead, (poetry) Pooka Press, BC, 2004 25 pp.

*How Beautiful We Are, (poetry) Souwesto Orion Prize, Black Moss Press, 2006 45 pp.

But Where Were the Horses of Evening, (poetry) Serengeti Press, 2007 35 pp.

Let Light Try All the Doors, Rubicon Press, (poetry) fall 2009 35 pp.

One Leaf in the Breath of the World, (poetry) Beret Days Press, 2009 35 pp.

Adoration of the Unnecessary, (poetry) Beret Days Press, 2015

My Sister Rides a Sorrow Mule (Beret Days Books, 2019)

This Darkness Born in Light, (Big Pond Rumours, 2019)

Riddle Me This (Hidden Brook Press, 2021)

Translation

Sweet Cuba: The Building of a Poetic Tradition: 1608-1958 (Hidden Brook Press, 2010 (in collaboration with co-translator Dr. Manuel de JesúsVelázquez León)

Editor

*That Sign of Perfection: From Bandy Legs to Beer Legs (poems and stories on the game of hockey), (anthology) Black Moss Press, 1995

*Losers First: poems and stories on game and sport, (anthology) Black Moss Press, 1999

*I Want to Be the Poet of Your Kneecaps: poems of quirky romance, (anthology) Black Moss Press, 1999

*Following the Plough: poems and stories on the land, (anthology) Black Moss Press, 2000

*Henry's Creature: poems and stories on the automobile, (anthology co-edited with Roger Bell) Black Moss Press, 2000

*Smaller Than God: words of spiritual longing, (anthology co-edited with Brother Paul Quenon) Black Moss Press, 2001

*Body Language: a head-to-toe anthology, (anthology) Black Moss Press, 2003

Witness: anthology of war poetry, (anthology) Serengeti Press, Mississauga, Ontario, 2004

Bonjour Burgundy, (anthology) Mosaic Press, 2008

*Under the Weight of Heaven, (anthology) Black Moss Press, 2008

*Tough Times: an anthology of essays on the state of the arts in tough economic times, edited by John B. Lee (Black Moss Press, 2010)

*Decabration: the tenth anniversary anthology of The Ontario Poetry Society, Beret Days Books, 2011

When the Full Moon Comes: writing from Santiago de Cuba (Hidden Brook Press, 2012)

An Unfinished War: poems and stories on the War of 1812 (Black Moss Press, 2012)

Beyond the Seventh Morning (Sandcrab, 2012)

Window Fishing: the night we caught Beatlemania, (Hidden Brook Press, 2014) second edition 2015, extended play edition 2016

Alice Munro: A Souwesto Celebration, (edited by J.R. (Tim) Struthers and John B. Lee, (Windsor Review, Fall, 2014)

Because We Have Lived Here: Poems Along the South Shore, (Black Moss Press, 2017)

The Beauty of Being Elsewhere, (Hidden Brook Press, 2021)

John B. Lee Signature Series (Hidden Brook Press) selected for publication and edited by John B. Lee

An Evening Absence Still Waiting for Moon, Bruce Kaufman (John B. Lee Signature Series, Hidden Brook Press, 2019)

The Star-Brushed Horizon, Don Gutteridge (John B. Lee Signature Series, Hidden Brook Press, 2019)

Out of Darkness, Light, April Bulmer (John B. Lee Signature Series, Hidden Brook Press, 2019)

Home Ground, Don Gutteridge (John B. Lee Signature Series, Hidden Brook Press, 2019)

Conditions of Desire, John Di Leonardo (John B. Lee Signature Series, Hidden Brook Press, 2019)

Whatever We Are, Eva Kolacz (John B. Lee Signature Series, Hidden Brook Press 2019)

Forthcoming from the John B. Lee Signature Series

New Collected Poems: 1957-2017, Robert Sward (John B. Lee Signature Series, Hidden Brook Press, 2020)

Listen to People, John Tyndall (John B. Lee Signature Series, Hidden Brook Press, 2020)

The Mezzo-Soprano Dines Alone, Tom Gannon Hamilton (Hidden Brook Press, 2020)

Still Dancing, Michael Wilson (John B. Lee Signature Series, Hidden Brook Press, 2022)

Marty Gervais, (John B. Lee Signature Series, Hidden Brook Press, 2022)

Robyn Butt, (John B. Lee Signature Series, Hidden Brook Press, 2022)

That Isn't You, John B. Lee (selected by publisher Richard Grove as the capstone of the John B. Lee Signature Series, 2022)

*my work has been published internationally in over 500 anthologies, journals, magazines

Forthcoming

That Isn't You spring 2022

Work-in-progress

A School Called Normal (a series of poems and stories on school)
A Wet Wild Seed in the Hot Blind Earth, (forthcoming from Red Maple Press in Bangladesh)
In the Arc Welder's Blinding Light

American Poetry Association's Annual Poetry Award, 1st place,

1985 Cross-Canada Writer's Quarterly, 2nd Runner Up,

1988 Roundhouse Poetry Award, 1st place,

1989 and 1990 The Nova Scotia Poetry Award, 1st place,

1989 Charterhouse Poetry Award of London England, short-list,

1990 CBC Radio Literary Award for Poetry, 2nd place,

1990 **Milton Acorn Memorial People's Poetry Award, Runner-up 1987, Winner 1993 and 1995**

The League of Canadian Poets Competition, Honourable Mention,

1993 Matrix Magazine Travel Writing Award, 1st Place,

1994 **The Tilden Award, (CBC Radio/Saturday Night Magazine), Winner,**

1995 Confederation Poetry Award, Honourable Mention,

1995 Humanitas Poetry Award, Honourable Mention,

1995 Canadian Writer's Journal Poetry Award, Honourable Mention,

1995 The Tilden Award, short list,

1996 People's Poetry Award, winner,

1996 Milton Acorn Memorial People's Poetry Award, short list,

1996 Arc Magazine Best Poem Award, Honourable Mention,

1996 Petro-Canada Poet Laureate,

1996 CBC Literary Awards, short list,

1997 Trillium Awards, Nominee,

1996 and 1997 Canadian Author's Association Literary Awards, Nominee,

1996 and 1997 Leacock Poetry Award,

top-ten, 1997 O.A.C. Works in progress grants, 1993, 1994, 1995,

1996 Frith Press Chapbook Award, Honourable Mention,

1997 Acorn-Rukeyser Chapbook Award, short-list,

1998 Sandburg Livesay Short list,

1997 and 1998 People's Political Poem Award, winner,

Winter 1997 Amethyst Magazine Harbour Writing Award, winner,

1997 Fiddlehead Magazine Poetry Award, short-list,

1998 Milton Acorn Memorial People's Poetry Award, short-list

1998 This Magazine's Great Canadian Literary Hunt, Honourable Mention,

1998 The Canadian Literary Awards, short list (CBC radio/Saturday Night, 1998) People's Poetry Award, nominee,

1999 Canadian Author's Association Poetry Book Award, nominee,

1999 b p Nichol Chapbook Award, nominee,

1999 Pushcart Prize, Nominee,

1999 Literary Network News, Top Ten Canadian Poetry books, winter

1999 Literary Network News, Top Five Canadian Poetry chapbooks,

spring 1999 University of Windsor Review Poetry Prize, third place,

2000 Cranberry Tree Press Poetry award, first place,

2000 Lexikon Poetry Award,

2000 Sandburg Livesay Poetry Award, Honourable Mention,

2000 Milton Acorn Memorial People's Poetry Award, short-list

1999-2000 Editor's Prize Open Window II

ShauntBasmajian Chapbook Award Short list,

2003 The Great Canadian Literary Hunt, short list,

2003 Canadian Literary Award short list,

2002 Certificate of Excellence for outstanding achievement in litera-
     ture, Ridgetown District High School Hall of Fame, April 28,

2002 Ontario Poetry Society Life Member,

2002 Eric Hill Award of Literary Excellence in poetry,

 Qwerty magazine and University of New Brunswick, spring 2003

 Ontario Poetry Society chapbook award Honourable Mention,

2003 Eric Hill Award of Literary Excellence in poetry, Qwerty magazine and
     University of New Brunswick,

2005 CV2 poetry award, 2nd place,

2005 ShauntBasmajian chapbook award, First Runner Up,

2005 Acorn Rukeyser chapbook award, short list,

2005 Canadian Poetry Association Life Member Award,

2005 appointed Poet Laureate of Brantford,

2005 Souwesto/Orison Award,

2006 Acorn Plantos People's Poetry Award short list,

2006 CBC Literary Awards, short list,

2006 Tracking a Serial Poet, short list,

2006 Canada Council Writers' Grant, $20,000

(spring 2006) Vallum Poetry Award, 2nd prize,

spring 2006 Winston Collins/Descant magazine Best Canadian Poem Award

2007 Souwesto/Orison Award short list

2007 Cranberry Tree Press Honourable Mention

2007 Black Moss Press "Souwesto Award"

2008 2nd place in CV2 Erotic Poetry Competition

2008 Pablo Neruda Poetry Prize Vancouver Public library

2009 Golden Grassroots Chapbook Award

2009 Rubicon Press Chapbook Award

2009 Cranberry Tree Press Poetry Prize

2009 Petra Kenny Poetry Prize

2010 No Love Lost Poetry Prize

2010 Honourable Mention in Aeroborialis poetry competition

2010 Ascent Aspirations poetry prize honourable mention

2011 Second Chapter and Verse poetry competition winner

2012 Ascent Aspirations "Hunger on Bourbon Street" First Prize Poetry

2012 Raymond Souster Poetry Award nominee

2013 Let Us Be Silent Here, poetry collection, Sanbun Publishing Acorn/ Livesay People's Poetry Award

2013 Winston Collins/Descant Prize for the Best Canadian Poem

2014 Raymond Souster Poetry Award Nominee

2015 Golden Grassroots Chapbook Award Honourable Mention

2015 Cranberry Tree Press Chapbook Award Honourable Mention

2016 Dr. William Henry Drummond Poetry Contest first Honourable mention

2016 Scugog Arts Council Poetry Award First Place

2017 Hourglass Poetry Award First Place

2017 Literary Encyclopedia Award First Place

2017 Big Pond Rumours chapbook awards Honourable mention

2017 Canada 150 Medal Recipient

2019 The Golden Oracle: The Late Great Planet Rock Star Contest Winner

2019 The Golden Grassroots Chapbook Award for *My Sister Rides a Sorrow Mule*

2019 Big Pond Rumours Chapbook Award 1st Honourable Mention for *This Darkness Born in Light*

2019 Saving Bannister Poetry Award

2019 Dogwood Lifetime Achievement Award Norfolk County Heritage and Culture Dogwood Awards

2020 Poet Laureate of Canada Cuba Literary Association

2020 The Angela ConsoloMankiewicz*Poetry Award*

2020 Bannister Poetry Anthology Award First Place and First Honourable Mention

2021 3rd place in the Writing Spring Award, The Ontario Poetry Society

2021 The Angela ConsoloMankiewicz*Poetry Award*

2021 The Love Lies Bleeding Poetry Anthology Contest 3 Honourable Mentions

2021 Arthur Lefebvre Award for Excellence in Career Achievement by a Brantford Writer (Brantford Writers' Circle)
2021 Bannister Poetry Award 1st Place for the poem "In the Arc Welder's Blinding Light," and Honourable Mention for the poem "Unimportant Work"